Surviving McCoy

E. K. McCoy

Catherine,

Happy Reading ☺

E. K. McCoy

This book was inspired by my life. All of the stories are recreations from actual
events and do hold some truth. In order to maintain their anonymity I have, in
some instances, changed the names of individuals and places as well as identifying
characteristics and details such as physical properties, occupations, and places of
residence.

ISBN-13: 978-1979502771
ISBN-10: 1979502773

Front cover and interior design by Terry Bailey
Photography by Deborah Harvey
Photo editing by Andy Meyer

Printed in the United States of America
First Edition: November 2017

Acknowledgments

I am humbled in writing these acknowledgments because without the love and support of my family and friends, my dream of publishing a book would be just that—a dream. However, because of these precious ones, I am who I am today, and I found the courage and inspiration to make my dream a reality.

To my husband, KP—thank you for believing in me and for giving me the nudge I needed to follow my heart. While others might have laughed at me for saying I wanted to quit my job to focus on writing, you said, "I couldn't agree more. Do it!" Thank you for being my biggest supporter. Thank you for taking care of the girls for hours (or sometimes days) whenever I was in the mood to write. Thank you for never complaining whenever I kept you up late asking your opinion and re-reading the same sentence to you again and again until it was just right. Every day you inspire me to be the best version of myself, and the girls and I are extremely lucky to have you in our lives.

Everything I have accomplished in life is a result of the way my mom and dad loved me, raised me, and supported me. They taught me from a very young age that anything was possible as long as I was willing to work hard and remain dedicated. They inspired me to do my best and reassured me that I could accomplish anything I set my mind to. They kept me grounded and level-headed through my teen years, teaching me never to be too proud and to always care for others. And as I navigated some very challenging years as a young adult, they lavished me with love, support, and encouragement when I needed it most. Without them, I couldn't have earned my college degree, bought my first home, or become the person I am today. Mom, Dad—I owe you everything.

This book truly would not have been possible without my sisters. "Charlie" and "Liz"—thank you for such a crazy, unique, fun-filled childhood. I hold close to my heart the memory of every family vacation, summer and holiday break, and even our everyday grind. This book is dedicated to our lives as "McCoy Boys." Each day with you was an adventure. You should know that I've always looked up to you. Charlie—I admire your determination to achieve anything you set your mind to, your courage to venture wherever your heart leads, and your love for life. (Sorry I made you out to be the bad guy.) Liz—growing up, you always protected Charlie and me. You were our role model and my mini-mommy. As an adult, I admire your determination to make a difference in the lives of every child you teach, your honesty, your passion to do good, and your love for life.

To my daughters, Ellie and Ava, who remind me daily to live life to its fullest—your tiny mommy loves you dearly. Thank you for making me laugh and smile and for filling my heart with more love than I ever knew was possible. It was your childlike wonder that inspired me to fill these pages with stories of my own childhood.

Cheryl—you are the mother-in-law every woman dreams of having. Thank you for your love and support throughout this long book writing and publishing process. For you there was never any question as to whether I could finish; rather it was always "when you finish." Gerald—your story of becoming an author inspired me. When I was questioning my decision to publish, you reassured me that I have a voice and that people need to hear it. Thank you for your guidance and especially for introducing me to Terry, my editor. Terry—you are incredible to work with. Not only are you amazing with words, but you believed in me, encouraged me, and patiently walked this "newbie" step-by-step through unknown territory. Thank you taking such good care of my "baby" and for transforming my rough manuscript into a finished book that my family and I will treasure for all of our lives.

To my grandparents, aunts, uncles, and cousins—I truly love you. Thank you for being there for me through thick and thin. Thank you for all the good times we've had playing cards on Christmas Eve, taking fun vacations, and for every time we've gathered as a family. My cousins were my first playmates, and to this day are some of my closest friends. Although we lost Poppy, Apple, Grandma and Grandpa McCoy, Uncle "Hudy," Great Aunt Pat, and Aunt Kris along the way, they live on in our hearts and in the stories we share.

And last but not least are my Deer Park friends whom I have known since childhood. We grew up together and have shared laughter and tears. Throughout the years you have loved me for who I am and remain always just a phone call or text away. Thank you for that. I cherish our friendship.

Contents

Prologue...9

Unwanted from the Start.................................13

Someone Wants Me..17

We Are Flintstone Kids....................................21

Preschool: I Quit!..27

And a Gasp of Horror Fell over the Crowd....33

Milkshakes: Doctor's Orders...........................37

Speak Now or Forever Hold Your Pee...........43

Sharks and Nudists..51

Cry-Baby...63

Coney Island..69

A Man and His Boat...75

McCoy Christmas Traditions..........................83

The Scrooge Sisters..89

The Day the Game Went too Far..................107

Snap, Crackle, Pass Out................................113

Croquet, Anyone?...119

My Very Own Space.......................................129

Flash the Wonder Fish...................................137

The Roof, the Roof, the Roof is—!..............149

McCoy for President.......................................159

"It's the End of the World as We Know It"....165

"The Times They Are a-Changin"..................173

"All the Single Ladies"...................................181

Secrets..187

The Next Eight Years......................................193

When One Door Closes, Dare to Dream!.....199

Present Day..203

Prologue

"Eat the worm pie, Em, or your blankie gets cut!" Charlie said angrily as she shoved my tear-stained face into the worm-infested mud pie and then back out again.

As soon as my face was out of the pie, I gasped for air then spit dirt out of my mouth. I wanted to wipe dirt from my face but couldn't. Not only did Charlie have me kneeling with my arms pinned behind my back but she was sitting on my calves to keep me from running away. I was trapped. Charlie was my puppeteer, and I was her submissive puppet. She controlled my every move.

Out of the corner of my eye I could see our oldest sister Liz holding my beloved green blanket in one hand while slowly running the long, sharp scissors up and down my fragile baby blanket with her other hand.

I had had my "green thing," as my sisters liked to call it, for as long as I can remember. It used to be lined with soft, white silk, but through the years I had rubbed the silk edges until there was none left to rub. My green thing had been my source of comfort and security. During thunderstorms I'd hide under it. When I was sad, I'd bury my face in it and cry myself to sleep. I had taken it on every vacation and had secretly packed it in my pillowcase for every slumber party. Since both of my sisters had their own baby blankets that they cherished as much as I cherished mine, I thought we had an unspoken rule: we don't mess with one another's blankets. Apparently I was wrong to assume that mine was safe from their wrath.

"Tick-tock, Em, you're running out of time," Charlie warned as she impatiently pressed my face closer to the mud pie.

"I'm sorry, Charlie!" I cried as I thought back to the other day when Kelsey, Charlie's best friend, had been hanging out at our house. We were all eating a snack in the kitchen when I accidentally mentioned that Charlie wanted Tom to ask her to the upcoming dance. Little did I know that Kelsey had already asked Tom to go with her, and to make matters worse, Kelsey and Tom were now girlfriend and boyfriend! Needless to say, I had not only unintentionally humiliated Charlie but my little slip-up had caused a huge argument between Charlie and Kelsey. Charlie wasn't one to embarrass easily, but anyone who did embarrass her would pay dearly for having made her feel foolish, which is exactly why I found myself in the situation I was in.

"I didn't know Tom was Kelsey's boyfriend!" I pleaded.

"Too late! Snip a corner, Liz!" Charlie commanded. And just like that, I heard the loud snip of the scissors cutting through my poor, helpless blanket.

I let out a whimper and hoped that Liz had taken pity on the green thing and not cut too much off. I didn't understand why Charlie was being so mean or why Liz was helping her with this cruel and unusual punishment. Charlie would punch me, pick on me, and occasionally tie me to a chair, but she had never done anything this bad. Normally Liz would try to stop Charlie whenever she went too far, but today, like a dog following its owner's commands, Liz was doing whatever Charlie told her to do. The only logical explanation was that Charlie must have bribed or threatened her.

"Time's up, Hemi!" Charlie said as she began to shove my face back into the mud.

"All right! All right!" I cried harder. With my face only about an inch from the ground Charlie finally stopped shoving. "I'll do whatever you want! Just please don't cut any more!" I cried.

Charlie rammed my face forcefully back into the worm pie and held it there long enough for me to feel the slimy worms squirming across my closed eyes and lips. As I continued to hold my breath I felt one of them try to wiggle up my nose, and I began to panic. Luckily Charlie released her grip on me before the worm could squirm inside. As my head flew backwards I opened my mouth and gasped for air. I wiped mud from my eyes and nose and spit dirt out of my mouth and back onto the ground where it belonged.

Charlie stood up. "There's a list of chores lying on your bed. And next time you better think twice before talking to *my* friends!" And with that she stomped away.

Liz held her head low as she shamefully handed me a tissue and, with guilt-filled eyes, apologized. "I'm sorry, Em," she said as she laid my blanket on the ground beside me and added, "I only cut a tiny piece off."

"Liz!" Charlie screamed from the back porch, "No fraternizing with the enemy!"

Liz turned and walked away sulking.

I cried as I blew my nose into the tissue trying to get all the dirt out. All I could smell and taste was dirt and worms. Once I finished cleaning myself off as much as I could with just one tissue, I picked up my blanket and examined it. I let out a sigh of relief when I realized Liz had told the truth; she had only cut off a small corner piece.

To fully understand the dynamics of our relationship and how my sisters could get away with treating me this way, one would have to go way back to the beginning—my beginning.

Unwanted from the Start

The year was 1984, and the McCoy family was anxiously awaiting the arrival of their last child. Well, Mom and Dad were anxiously awaiting; oldest sister Elizabeth (Liz) and younger sister Charlotte (Charlie) were less than excited to be welcoming a sibling.

To four-year-old Liz another sibling meant sharing her things and having less time with Mom and Dad. Two-year-old Charlie didn't understand how her life was about to change, but she knew she didn't like the new crib that had invaded her room. All she cared about was getting a puppy.

On July 21, 1984, I was born—purplish-blue with the cord wrapped around my neck and gasping for air. "It's a girl!" the doctor announced as he untangled the cord from around my neck, and I let out my first cry for help. As my proud parents gazed lovingly at their third and final daughter, they gave me the name Emily. A few days later, Mom and I were released from the hospital, and Dad drove us to our home on Glenbury Lane, where I would meet my sisters for the first time.

Liz eagerly ran to the door to greet Mom and Dad. She hugged their legs as she looked up at them and smiled. "You're home!" she beamed.

"Yes, and we brought your sister home with us," Mom smiled back as she leaned down for Liz to see me.

"Tiny baby doll," Liz grinned.

"Yes, Emily is small," Mom agreed and then added, "and very fragile. We have to be careful with her."

"Come play tea party with my dolls," Liz insisted as she tugged on Mom's leg.

"No, sweetie," Dad said, "Emily's just a baby; she isn't yet old enough to play. We have to hold her and take care of her."

"Daddy, come play," Liz pouted as she folded her arms on her chest.

"I will in a little while, but right now I have to help Mom and Emily get settled in," Dad explained as he tried to give Liz a hug. But Liz was mad at Dad for not playing with her, so instead of hugging him she quickly turned away and stomped back to the corner of the room where her tea party and dolls were.

Mom and Dad looked at each other with concern. "That could have gone better," Dad said. Mom nodded in agreement.

Charlie, on the other hand, took an immediate interest in me. Standing on her tippy-toes, she eagerly grabbed at Mom's arms where I lay. Mom was delighted to bend down to Charlie's level so she could see me up close.

Charlie took one look at me and squealed excitedly, "Puppy!" I had been home for five minutes, and already Charlie had declared me Skittles, the puppy she had been asking Mom and Dad for.

Mom chuckled and said, "No, Charlie, she's your baby sister, Emily."

Charlie looked at me again and then back at Mom, shook her head no, and said, "Puppy, Momma, puppy!"

Mom looked to Dad indicating it was his turn to try explaining the situation to Charlie. "Emily is your baby sister, Charlie; she's not a puppy."

Again Charlie shook her head no then started clapping her hands and jumping up and down. "Skittles puppy!"

Even though Liz wanted nothing to do with me, she couldn't help but laugh. She thought it was hilarious that Charlie believed I was a puppy, and she quickly joined in on the fun. "Yes, Charlie, our new puppy, Skittles!" she encouraged. The first game my sisters taught me to play was fetch. They'd toss a bouncy ball and watch me crawl after it. When I crawled past them, they would pat me on my head as if I was their puppy.

There's nothing like raising three strong-willed girls, especially when the first two never wanted the third. No matter how many times Mom and Dad told Liz and Charlie that I was their sister Emily, not their dog, my sisters ignored them. From my birth on, my parents would be out-numbered.

Someone Wants Me

After having me, Mom quit her job to stay at home and raise us girls while Dad worked full time. Raising three children in middle-class Ohio on Dad's income alone was difficult. Any event or meal that was free was music to my parents' ears. So when our local park started hosting free children's movies, Mom took an immediate interest even if it meant dragging out her one-month-old, four-year-old, and two-year-old all by herself.

It was a typical hot and humid August day when Mom took us all to the park. With sweat dripping down her face, she struggled to pull Liz's long, beautiful blond hair back into a ponytail while simultaneously keeping restless Charlie close to her side and keeping an eye on me sitting in my pumpkin seat.

That day the park was particularly crowded. As Mom was putting Liz's hair up, Charlie impatiently took off towards the swings. Mom didn't waste a moment running after her, grabbing her only a few feet away. However, when she turned back around, she saw Liz standing in her same spot but didn't see me or my seat. Panic overtook Mom as she realized her worst fear had just become reality: she had lost her child! But I was too young to have run away; I had been taken—kidnapped!

Frantically Mom began scanning the crowd, looking to her left and then to her right, searching for someone carrying a pumpkin seat. When she didn't see me, she screamed, "Help! Someone took my baby!"

Now, I will say this about the human race: we all have moments when we are caught up in our own lives, oblivious to the world around us, but if someone yells kidnapped, you had better believe everyone will stop what they're doing to help. And that's exactly what happened. Everyone froze in their places looking at our frazzled mother and waiting for someone to make the first move—everyone, that is, except for one man on a bicycle who didn't stop to look at Mom or to help. Instead he pedaled off in the opposite direction, getting farther and farther away but not very quickly. That's because he was steering with just one hand; in his other hand was a pumpkin seat!

"Stop that man!" Mom yelled. Then she scooped up Charlie in one arm then sprinted towards Liz and wrapped her hand securely around her wrist. With Charlie bobbing up and down in Mom's arms and Liz being dragged alongside her, Mom took off as fast as she could. Charlie and Liz were scared. Mom never yelled unless one of them was in big trouble, and she never ran unless she was running after one of them to put them in the time-out chair. Charlie wrapped her arms tighter around Mom's neck holding on for dear life. Liz was being whipped around like a rag doll. People who were around us now had been too far away to have heard Mom yell kidnapped, so they were unaware that she was trying to rescue her baby from the man on the bike. As the crowd thinned, the man picked up speed, and the distance between Mom and him quickly grew larger. The farther away we got from the original crowd, the fewer were the people who knew what was going on.

As Mom reached the end of the park—out of breath and dripping sweat from running half a mile while holding Charlie and dragging Liz—she nearly collapsed when she spotted the bike lying on the ground in front of her. The back wheel was slowly spinning, and beside the bike sat my empty pumpkin seat.

"No!" she screamed over Charlie and Liz's crying. She quickly skimmed the crowd. "There!" At the far end of the park was a man sitting on a swing holding me.

"My baby!" Mom gasped in horror as she put Charlie down. She looked at Liz and Charlie—both of their faces stained with tears. They knew something bad was happening, and they were terrified. Mom took Liz's hand and put Charlie's smaller hand in hers. "Liz," she said in a stern voice so Liz would do exactly what she was told to do, "I need you to hold onto Charlie, and I need the both of you," she paused and looked at Charlie to make sure she was listening, "to stay right here as still as statues. Understand?" Liz nodded her head as Charlie stood still sniffling.

Mom released their hands from her sweaty palms, stood, turned, and began to sprint towards the swings. She glanced back every now and then to make sure Liz and Charlie were still in their spots.

As she approached the swing, she slowed down, and the man looked up at her. "Baby doll!" he said as he rocked me a little too forcefully. Immediately Mom could tell the man was mentally disabled, and she knew she needed to stay calm and think quickly in order to get me back safely.

"What's that you're holding?" Mom asked the man, trying to hide the terror in her voice.

"Baby doll!" he excitedly exclaimed as he proudly held me out towards Mom to show her. I was sound asleep. Mom's heart quickened as I wobbled in the man's arms. Mom feared the man would drop me at any moment.

"What a pretty doll!" she said.

"Yes, pretty!" he smiled as he patted my head with one hand.

"May I hold your baby doll?" Mom asked. Her legs wobbled as she took another step closer.

"Mine!" he said as he drew me in towards his chest. His sudden movement startled me, and I woke up and began to cry. My crying surprised the man. "No cry!" he shouted at me.

Mom took three swift steps closer to the man, closing the distance between the two of them. "I'm a mom," she calmly explained to him. "Let me see if I can get her to stop crying," she begged.

"Here!" he said as he forcefully threw me into Mom's arms. As I bobbled to and fro, Mom held onto me for dear life. Once she had a secure hold on me, she turned away from the man, and with weak legs quickly got as far away from him as possible. She dropped to the ground holding me as tightly as she could without hurting me, reassuring herself that her nightmare was over; I was safe in her arms. Now she could no longer hold back the tears. She began to cry hysterically as she rocked me—her screaming newborn who had no idea what I had just lived through. She motioned for Charlie and Liz, who weren't far away, to come to her so she could wrap her arms around all three of us.

Moments later, security guards took the man into custody. We spent the rest of the night in Children's Hospital where I was evaluated for any signs of injury; luckily, I was not injured. (This would be my family's first of many trips to the emergency room.) Mom and Dad decided not to press charges against the man who had taken me, given his mental disability, but he was banned from the local park. That was the last time Mom ever took us to the park alone.

Interestingly, I am not the only one in my family who has been kidnapped. At the age of five, my grandmother Apple Betty, who had an uncanny resemblance to Shirley Temple, was taken by a neighbor and tied to a chair in the basement. Luckily, she too was found unharmed.

When my oldest daughter was studying heredity in third grade, she raised her hand and shared nonchalantly with the class: "Kidnapping runs in my family, but it skips a generation. So I'm safe, but if I have kids, they'll probably get stolen."

We Are Flintstone Kids

Growing up, my sisters and I played rough, and throughout the years we were known to have several fist fights. A day didn't pass without one of us ending up with a new scratch or bruise, and we certainly had our fair share of stitches. We were always covered in dirt. We played and fought like boys, but we held grudges and sought revenge like girls. Our grandfather Poppy gave us the nickname The McCoy Boys.

The roughest, strongest, and most destructive of us all was Charlie, but what made her especially dangerous was her wit. She was often the mastermind behind all our crazy ideas and sneaky plans.

One day while Mom was cooking dinner, we were playing a game in the family room. (We often played there because the family room was connected to the kitchen, and there Mom could keep her eye on us while she was cooking.) Liz and Charlie had spread magazines all over the tile floor and were imagining the magazines were lily pads in a big, scary swamp full of mean alligators. In the swamp, the most annoying alligator—that was me—was chasing after them. The lily pads were their safe zone, and I had to catch them as they jumped from lily pad to lily pad. (Ever since my sisters stopped referring to me as Skittles and allowed me to play with them—allowed meaning Mom and Dad forced them to include me—I was immediately labeled the bad guy, and I would remain the bad guy for the rest of our childhood. For some reason I listened to them and would do whatever they told me to do. Why? Because I was the youngest, and if I didn't, they would torture me.)

My sisters shrieked with excitement as they leaped from lily pad to lily pad trying to escape my grasp. I caught Liz several times but hadn't yet caught Charlie (she was the fastest of us McCoy Boys). I was only three years old, but I was determined to catch her.

I was hot on Charlie's trail and apparently too close for her liking. As we passed in mid-air, she gave me a forceful push towards Liz that sent me flying across the floor. My foot slipped on a magazine, which catapulted my tiny body through the air. Before falling face down on the hard tile floor, my cheek caught the sharp corner of the TV stand.

Instantly all I could feel was pain, and all I could taste was blood. My two front teeth had gone straight through my lower lip. Mom rushed to my rescue and swooped me up into her loving arms as I screamed in pain. She took one look at my face and shouted, "Oh my goodness! Liz! Charlie! Get your shoes on now!"

She carried me into the kitchen to turn off the stove then straight up to the bathroom where she sat me on the toilet, grabbed a wash cloth, and pressed it hard against my cheek. Now I was really screaming! Until that moment I was unaware that I had even hurt my cheek. "There, there, Em," Mom hugged me with one arm as she held the washcloth with the other, "you hurt your cheek, but don't worry; it can be fixed. Mommy's here for you," she reassured me. Moments later we all piled into our minivan, and Mom drove us to the ER.

With an abundance of candy she had bought from the vending machine Mom bribed Charlie and Liz to sit quietly while the doctor examined me. After they glued my bottom lip back together, the nurse held me down while the doctor stitched four stitches into my right cheek. With each stitch I cried harder and harder as my sisters sat eating candy bar after candy bar and watching me kick and scream. (Through the years this would be the way my childhood unfolded—me being hurt while my sisters went unpunished or found pleasure in my pain.) To this day, I still have a scar on my right cheek to remind me of that spring day when magazines were lily pads and Charlie sent me flying.

* * *

A few weeks later, Mom made a mistake she would never make again. She left us unsupervised during breakfast to take a quick phone call. That morning as we were finishing our eggs and toast, the phone rang. At first Mom ignored it figuring whoever it was would leave a message; however, when the caller persisted, she determined it must be important, so she ran upstairs to answer the phone.

All Charlie needed was a minute to set any plan into action, and Charlie always had plans and ideas stored away just waiting for the perfect moment to implement them. This was the opportunity she'd been waiting for to activate her eat-all-the-candy-I-can-as-fast-as-I-can-without-Mom-knowing plan.

As soon as Mom was out of the kitchen and heading upstairs, Charlie was jumping down from her barstool and pushing it over to the kitchen cabinet as fast as her little legs could move. Once the chair was where she wanted it, she darted to the kitchen drawer, grabbed a spatula, ran back to the barstool and climbed on top, and then onto the kitchen counter. Standing securely on the counter, she opened the cabinet, stood on her tippy-toes, and used the spatula to reach the Flintstones Vitamins, which sat on the top shelf, way out of our reach.

"What are you doing?" Liz asked from the breakfast bar where we both sat eating our eggs and watching Charlie.

"Gettin' the vitamins—duh," Charlie whispered back at Liz.

Now, candy wasn't given to us hyperactive McCoy Boys often, except when Mom or Dad was using it as a bribe—as in hospital waiting rooms—and desserts and treats were saved for special occasions. Even sugary cereals and fruit snacks were a rarity in our house. So every morning when Mom gave us our Flintstones Vitamins, we would gratefully and slowly savor the delicious, sweet taste of that vitamin. It was more than a vitamin to us; it was as close as we would get to having candy on a daily basis.

"Almost there," Charlie said as she jumped and swatted the bottle of vitamins with the spatula. At last the bottle came flying down at Charlie, hit her in the chest, and then landed on the counter next to her feet. Once Charlie was standing back on the kitchen floor, she turned to show us her prize. She beamed as she proudly held the bottle out in front of her as if she had just found the golden egg at our family's Easter egg hunt.

So far everything was going according to plan. Mom must have forgotten to tighten the lid because with one swift twist of the "child-proof" lid the bottle opened, and Charlie jumped for joy. She poured a handful of vitamins into her small palm and excitedly popped them into her mouth all at once. As she chewed her mouthful of vitamins, I looked at Liz. Liz was smiling at Charlie and seemed rather amused. I didn't know what to do. I was too young to understand why Mom only gave us one a day; I only knew that it was Mom's rule, and when we broke Mom's rules, we got into big trouble.

I stopped eating my breakfast and watched Charlie give Liz multiple handfuls of vitamins. "Here, Em," Charlie said as she put several on the plate in front of me. I looked down at the delicious vitamins and then back at my sisters. They seemed to be okay after eating more than one—and they were being nice and sharing— so I decided to eat them.

A moment later, we heard the creaking of the stairs and knew Mom was on her way back down. "Hide the bottle!" Liz instructed Charlie. Charlie looked at the bottle and decided she wasn't quite ready to part with her beloved vitamins, so instead of hiding the bottle she decided to hide in the bathroom and continue eating. Liz quickly put the rest of her vitamins in her mouth, and I froze in place.

Mom came back into the kitchen and said, "Finish eating, girls; we're going to be late." I still had five vitamins on my plate and didn't know what to do. I put my napkin over my plate—a trick I'd watched Liz and Charlie do whenever Mom said they couldn't leave the table without eating all their broccoli—and hoped Mom wouldn't see the vitamins.

"Where's Charlie?" Mom asked Liz as she picked up the OJ from the breakfast bar and put it back in the refrigerator.

"Uhhh... I think in the bathroom," Liz said, staring down at her plate and avoiding eye contact with Mom.

Mom turned her attention to me. "Are you finished, Em?" I nodded my head yes as Mom reached for my plate. Even at the age of three, I knew that once Mom saw those vitamins on my plate, I was in trouble.

As soon as Mom began cleaning my plate, she saw the vitamins and immediately panicked. "Liz, where did Emily get these vitamins, and how many did she eat?" Liz sat there quietly, still avoiding eye contact with Mom. She knew she was in trouble and was trying to think of something clever to say. Before Liz had time to think of a lie, Mom put two and two together and screamed, "Charlie!" as she ran to the bathroom. The door was locked. She banged on the door. "Charlie, I know you're in there, and I know you have the vitamins. Open this door right now!"

Silence filled the kitchen as Liz and I waited to see what Mom would do to Charlie.

Charlie didn't answer Mom.

"Charlie? Open the door, Charlie!"

Nothing. Charlie was completely silent.

Mom ran to the junk drawer, grabbed the screwdriver, and ran back to the bathroom door. She used the screwdriver to pop the lock on the door. As soon as Mom opened the door, she saw Charlie sitting on the toilet seat holding the Flintstones bottle and grinning from ear to ear with vitamin pieces covering her face and mouth. Mom snatched the bottle from Charlie's hand. To her horror, the bottle was completely empty.

"Oh, no!" Mom cried as she swooped up Charlie from the seat and came back to the kitchen. She sat Charlie down on the barstool. "Liz, I need to know how many you and Emily ate, and I need to know now," Mom demanded.

"Why are you yelling at me? I didn't do anything wrong; Charlie did, " Liz said as she folded her arms over her chest.

"You are the oldest, and you are not in trouble; Charlie is," Mom said as she looked towards Charlie and gave her a stern look, "but I need to know because you can get sick if you eat too many, and the bottle is empty!"

"Sick?" Liz asked as she looked to Charlie.

"Yes," Mom nodded.

Liz started to cry. "I ate a few handfuls. Charlie made me!" she screamed as she pointed at Charlie. Charlie's grin quickly disappeared from her face. Moments ago, she was savoring her victory, and now all she was worried about was what Mom meant when she said you can get sick from eating too many vitamins.

"Okay, everyone put their shoes on," Mom ordered as she helped me down from my chair and gave both Liz and Charlie a loving pat on the back reassuring them that everything was going to be fine.

Moments later, we all piled into the minivan and once again headed to Children's emergency room. This time I was the one sitting in the chair eating candy while the doctors examined Liz and Charlie. My, how the tables had turned in just two short weeks. Liz was given some nasty substance to drink that made her vomit. No one knew exactly how many vitamins Charlie had eaten.

As we waited for Dad to arrive, the doctors made the decision to have Charlie's stomach pumped. After that day, Charlie cringed at the sight, taste, and smell of vitamins. Mom and Dad worried that after two trips in two weeks to Children's Hospital, it was only a matter of time before social services would come knocking on our door.

As we got older, whenever a Flintstones Vitamins commercial would come on TV, Liz and I would sing their theme song loudly in Charlie's general direction. Even though Charlie would sometimes throw us a wicked punch for reminding her of the day she had her stomach pumped, seeing the sickening look on her face was worth the pain.

Preschool: I Quit!

When I was three, Mom went back to work part-time. On the days she worked, I'd spend the day at my grandparents Apple and Poppy's house. The days passed easily there sitting on Poppy's lap in his big, blue velvet recliner eating Oreos while we watched *The Price is Right*. Not only were Oreo cookies a daily snack for me but Apple and Poppy would often spoil me by taking me to my favorite ice cream parlor, Graeter's, for an afternoon treat. Yes, while Liz and Charlie were at school, I would spend my days eating cookies and ice cream and watching TV. Ah, the perks of being three and having no responsibilities. On weekends our family would gather at Apple and Poppy's house for Sunday night dinner. Most weeks I was at their house at least four out of seven days. Needless to say, I was very close to both of them.

When I turned four, my life took a dramatic turn. Not only was Poppy diagnosed with lung cancer but Mom and Dad decided to enroll me in all-day preschool, and I was furious. Although I didn't understand what being sick with cancer meant, I was mad that Poppy was sick, and angry with my parents for making me go to school. My days were supposed to be spent with my grandparents at the park, zoo, or at Graeter's—not at school. I didn't want to go to school with Liz and Charlie. I had grown accustomed to spending time with Apple and Poppy and having time away from my sisters.

Every day when Mom dropped us off at school, Liz and Charlie would jump out of the minivan while I would throw a royal temper tantrum and refuse to get out of my booster seat. Mom would practically drag me out of the van and into the classroom. Instead of hugging and kissing Mom goodbye, I'd fold my arms across my chest, fling my pigtails, and deliver my famous line: "You can make me go to school, but you can't make me learn!" I'd sass as I'd turn and stomp my way into the classroom.

Every night at the dinner table when Mom and Dad would ask about my school day, I would complain: "They want me to color, cut, *and* paste all in the same day," I'd pout, "It's exhausting!" or "They want me to learn how to spell my name *and* my address. Can you believe those teachers?!"

Liz and Charlie would laugh at me and warn me that school would only get harder. They told me that after next year those mean teachers would take away my nap and snack time and give me homework. I couldn't believe it. The nerve of those teachers! Making me learn was one thing, but taking away my nap and snack time?! I don't think so! I didn't want anything to do with them or school!

Although I didn't like going to school to learn, I had a secret that I was keeping from my family: I liked going to school to make friends, and I had made several of them. It was nice to play with kids who didn't beat me up or pick on me the way Liz and Charlie did. Also I learned that if I was good and listened to my teacher, I'd get extra snacks and stickers during circle time, but I didn't want my parents to know this. After all, I had to make them feel bad about taking away my alone time with my grandparents.

As concerned parents, Mom and Dad set up a meeting with my teacher, Mrs. Miller, to discuss how I was doing in school. Mrs. Miller had nothing but great things to say about me, calling me "a pleasure to have in class" and reassuring them that I had plenty of friends and was happy at school. My parents were shocked to discover my secret. They sat me down and explained that Mrs. Miller thought I was doing very well in school, and they asked me to stop throwing daily fits. This only made things worse as now I was furious with Mrs. Miller for telling my parents my secret.

As the days passed, I continued my daily temper tantrums and nightly dinnertime complaints. By Christmas break, Poppy had taken a turn for the worse, and my parents—too emotionally exhausted to deal with three kids and Mom's dying father—gave into my daily tantrums and decided to remove me from preschool.

"Preschool dropout!" Liz and Charlie would tease, but I didn't care. Sure, I'd miss my friends, but Mom had gotten their phone numbers and told me that we'd set up play dates. Now I'd get to play with friends at the park instead of at school; this was the best of both worlds! And after Christmas break, I would return to the good life at Apple and Poppy's while Liz and Charlie would return to school and homework—or so I thought. I had no idea my life would soon be turned upside down.

Poppy was getting weaker by the day. Instead of sitting on his lap watching *The Price is Right*, I'd sit in the living room with Apple while Poppy took a nap. I was allowed in the back room on Poppy's lap only for a short time each day. As I'd sit on his lap, I'd trace the bald eagle tattoo on his arm. He told me he got it when he was a Marine fighting in Iwo Jima. I didn't know what that meant; all I knew was that as the days passed, his tattoo began to change. His arm went from muscular to thin, and his tattoo looked faded and wrinkly instead of bright and smooth.

By springtime, Poppy's and my roles had reversed. Instead of him spoon-feeding me Graeter's ice cream while I sat on his lap, I'd stand by his recliner and feed him ice cream from my bowl. I was too young to understand why he couldn't eat much anymore or play with me the way he used to. He used to hold me upside down and tickle my belly and chase me around the backyard; now he could hardly stand. All I knew was that I missed playing with him and sitting on his lap.

Sadly, Poppy would lose his battle to lung cancer. A week before he passed, his doctor had warned us that Poppy didn't have much time left, so the entire family gathered at my grandparents' house for nightly family dinners. Although he was weak, Poppy would sit at the head of the table and watch all nine grandkids eat.

Then after dinner he'd sit on the couch and watch us all play in the living room.

It was a Friday night when he left us. After dinner, all the kids had piled into Mom's minivan to go get ice cream, and we returned to find an ambulance in the driveway and the front door propped open. Although I was young, I didn't need my sisters or my parents to explain that the ambulance in the driveway meant bad news for Poppy.

Before the van had stopped moving, Cousin Jon and I tore off our seat belts, threw open the sliding door, and raced into the house. I was too focused on my destination to see my uncle Hudy embracing his wife Tess on the front porch or my aunt Carol holding Apple as she cried into her shoulder in the living room. I rounded the living room corner to work my way down the hall to Poppy's back room—the room where I would sit with him in his big, blue velvet recliner—but as soon as I rounded the corner, I realized the door was shut. Poppy never shut the door; he always wanted his grandkids to come in and sit on his lap. I stopped in my tracks. I didn't need an adult to tell me—I knew Poppy had died.

Cousin Jon took a step in front of me and then turned around to face me. His blue eyes pooled with tears as his pale, freckled face grew bright red with frustration. "He loved me the most!" he screamed in my face.

I had never felt like this before—sad, frustrated, scared, and angry all at once. Just like Cousin Jon, I too needed to take out these confusing emotions on someone, and that someone was Jon! Never mind that he was one month older than me and a whole head taller. My emotions took control of my body, and before I could process what I was doing, I had tackled him to the ground.

Taken by surprise, Jon lay lifeless underneath me, stunned as I smashed the remainder of my ice cream cone repeatedly into his face while he cried. But I didn't stop there. I angrily rubbed orange sorbet into his sandy blond curls while sobbing and screaming, "No, he loved me the most!" I don't know how long I continued to smack him and rub sticky orange sorbet all over his red, tear-stained face before Liz interrupted our he-loved-me-more fight.

"Stop it, Em!" Liz's voice from behind me broke my angry tirade as she wrapped her arms around me and tried to peel me off of Jon. I was holding onto him for dear life, refusing to let go. "Stop it!" she screamed louder and pulled me with all her might. We both went flying backwards onto the floor, and I finally released Jon from my death grip. Liz wrapped her arms and legs around me and held me in a bear hug as I lay on top of her crying. "It's going to be okay!" she tried to reassure me through her own tears. "We're going to be okay," she sobbed.

* * *

MISSING YOU
A Poem for Poppy

As I lie here in the grass
Talking quietly to you
I realize how long it's been
And how much I miss you.
I'm growing up and succeeding well
In everything I do
And if I ever feel I can't
I close my eyes and think of you.
I know you're watching over me
I can feel you all around
And on days like these the gentle breeze
Makes it feel as though you're smiling down.
Although it's hard to carry on
Continue day to day
I know in my heart we will never part
And I know, I'll see you again
Someday.

E. K. McCoy, age 10

And a Gasp of Horror
Fell over the Crowd

Ever since Poppy passed, Mom had been unusually quiet and also busy with Aunt Patti and Aunt Anne making all the funeral arrangements. During this time, us McCoy Boys were on our best behavior. We left one another alone—didn't argue and even sat lovingly on the couch next to one another as we binged on Disney movies to keep out of Mom and Dad's way.

Three days after Poppy passed, we all gathered to say our final goodbyes to Poppy. None of us complained to Mom or Dad about having to go to church or wear itchy, annoying dress tights. Liz, Charlie, and I were nervous, sad, and scared not knowing what to expect at the first funeral we had ever attended.

The night before, Mom had prepared me by explaining that Poppy would be lying very still in a big box called a casket and that we were all going to take turns walking up to the casket to say our final goodbyes to him. This was all very confusing to a four-year-old.

I knew how much Poppy loved all the pictures I would draw him and the letters I would "write" him, and I didn't want him to leave without one last picture from me. So I stayed up late drawing Poppy a picture and writing him a letter. I folded it into a small square and laid it next to my dress so I wouldn't forget it the next day.

In my sticky, sweaty palm I held my folded-up picture for Poppy as I approached the casket with my family. As Mom hugged Apple, Dad put his arm around both of them. Liz, being the oldest, was the first of us kids to approach the casket. She stepped up on the stool that had been placed by the head of his casket, kissed her fingers, touched them to Poppy's face, and then stepped down and stood to the side indicating it was Charlie's turn. Charlie followed Liz's lead, mimicking her every move, and then stepped to the side. It was my turn. I looked towards Mom and Dad for help, but they were still talking to Apple.

I took in a deep breath and told myself to be big and brave as my sisters had been. I nervously stepped up onto the stool, but I was so small that even standing on my tippy-toes I could barely reach Poppy. I took one look at his face and quickly looked away. He didn't look the same. He wasn't smiling back at me or reaching to pick me up to swing me around. This wasn't the happy, fun-loving Poppy I knew; he was too still. I started to panic. I didn't want to be on the stool anymore. I wanted to give him my drawing and go sit down.

With sweaty palms I tried to reach his suit pocket to place my drawing in it but just couldn't reach. I began to gently jump—pushing off of the stool to try to get closer—and as I did, the casket shook. My hand was almost there. I was focusing so hard on getting the drawing into his pocket that I didn't realize my tiny body had started to climb into the casket. Poppy began to move. Startled, I quickly moved backwards causing Poppy to move towards me. I couldn't move my feet quickly enough to get out of the casket and back onto the stool. I practically jumped backwards. And that's when it happened.

Apple shrieked, "No, Em!" as Dad quickly scooped me out of the falling casket and my uncles raced to catch it before it hit the floor. They weren't fast enough. The quiet church was suddenly filled with gasps of horror as poor Poppy's casket tipped over with a loud thud that echoed throughout the entire church.

I buried my head into Dad's chest and sobbed hysterically. I knew I had done something terribly wrong. As my uncles worked quickly to lay Poppy back to rest, Dad carried me over to Charlie and Liz and raced us to the back of the church as far away as possible from the horrid scene I had just created. Once we reached the back of the church, Liz and Charlie remained wide-eyed and quiet—most likely just as shocked as I was—and waited for Dad to lay into me.

"What were you doing?" Dad scolded as he tried to put me down on the ground to look me in the eyes. I fought back, clinging to him as hard as I could. I was crying too hard to answer. With my face still buried in his chest, I untucked my arm and opened my sweaty hand to let the drawing fall to the ground.

Dad tightened his one-armed grip around me as he bent down to pick up the folded piece of paper. Upon unfolding it, he instantly understood. "It's going to be okay," he reassured me, and he gave me a kiss on my head. "I understand now, and I know it was an accident," he said.

Charlie and Liz were confused, wondering why Dad was comforting me instead of killing me. Once my crying slowed down, Dad released his hold on me and said, "You wait here with your sisters," and handed me over to Liz. "I don't want you girls to move a single muscle or make a single peep until I get back," Dad instructed before he walked away.

We all watched curiously as Dad walked to the front of the church and whispered something into Apple's ear. Although Apple was still crying, she nodded her head in understanding and took my drawing from Dad's hand.

By this time Poppy was safe and sound back in his casket. Apple approached him, refolded my drawing, and then placed it into Poppy's pocket. As my drawing made it to its final resting place, I let out a sigh of relief.

After the funeral, we all gathered at Apple's house. While the kids played outside, the adults comforted Apple and made a big family dinner. Later that night after the crowd had left Apple's house, I sat quietly watching TV in Poppy's recliner. Apple came in, picked me up, sat me on her lap, and told me how much she and Poppy loved my picture. I hugged her tighter than I ever knew was possible. Apple was the best grandma. She never grew angry and always knew how to make everything better.

Milkshakes: Doctor's Orders

A couple of weeks after losing Poppy, Aunt Patti took us McCoy Boys out to dinner while Mom and Dad went to Apple's to help sort through the last of Poppy's belongings. We loved going to dinner with Aunt Patti. Not only would she let us order whatever we wanted but she'd let us drink Coke *and* buy us dessert! Soda pop was hard to come by in the McCoy household, and when Mom did let us drink pop, she'd water it down. I grew up calling Coke "cokey water." Although Patti didn't have any children of her own, she sure knew how to spoil her nieces and nephews.

Between Poppy's passing and this day, Liz and Charlie hadn't picked on me, making it the longest they had ever gone without being mean to me, stealing my toys, or torturing me just for the fun of it. They had been on their best behavior for far too long. They had pent-up energy, and I could see it in their eyes. Like predators ready to pounce on their prey, they were ready to sink their teeth into me the first chance they got.

Once our milkshakes and appetizers arrived at the table, Aunt Patti told us all to behave while she went to the bathroom. As soon as Patti was out of sight, Charlie bit into a cheese stick and pulled it far away from her mouth letting the warm cheese form a long, gooey strand. She blew on the cheese willing it to cool. Once it was cooled and hard enough, Charlie flung the strand of cheese across the table at my face and laughed as it hit me smack-dab in the eye. Instantly my eye stung.

I rubbed my eye but decided to ignore Charlie. I continued to mind my own business and drink my delicious chocolate milkshake.

I didn't know how long it would be until I got another one, so I needed to ignore my sisters and savor my shake.

Charlie was annoyed that smacking me in the eye with her strand of cheese hadn't fazed me, so she reached across the table and snatched my shake right out of my hand. In the process of stealing my shake, she spilled some of it onto the table, which angered me.

"Charlie, give me back my shake!" I commanded as I rubbed my eye again. It still stung and had begun to water.

Liz sat there grinning as she watched the fight unfold. (Like I said, it had been weeks since they had picked on me. Even Liz was ready for some sister drama.)

"No!" Charlie said with a smirk on her face.

"You have to earn it back!" Liz excitedly chimed in.

"How?" I pouted as I crossed my arms and stared at my shake.

"By entertaining us!" Charlie said as she looked at Liz and smiled.

From past experience I've learned that it's easier and faster for me if I just do what my sisters ask rather than fight them, so I agreed with a pouty "Fine!"

"I bet you your milkshake that you can't eat a whole cheese stick in one single bite," Charlie taunted me.

"Ew!" I said as I scrunched up my nose and tried not to gag. (Most kids love cheese sticks, but not me. Once Liz and Charlie thought it'd be fun to hold me down and force-feed me an entire can of Cheez Whiz. After several squirts of cheese, I began to gag, but they didn't stop. They continued to force the cheese down my throat until I was sick. I spent the whole night puking up bright orange, nasty-tasting imitation cheese. Since that night, cheese has been my enemy.)

Charlie could tell I needed some motivation, so she took a big, long sip of my chocolate shake, swallowed, and with loud "Mmmm" passed it to Liz. Liz followed her lead, but not only did she take a big sip of my shake; she scooped a spoonful of whipped cream off the top! My eyes widened in disappointment as

I watched my shake begin to disappear right before my eyes. God only knew when I'd get a chocolate milkshake again.

I took a deep breath, grabbed a cheese stick from Charlie's plate, and shoved the entire stick into my mouth. I held my nose as I started to chew. Holding my nose helped to lessen the disgusting taste in my mouth but also made it harder to breathe since my mouth was full. At that moment, all I cared about was getting my shake back.

The cheese stick I took was too big for my tiny mouth, but I was determined. My cheeks began to puff out more and more. Like a chipmunk trying to find the room to store more food, I continued to pocket the chewed-up cheese stick in my mouth until I started having trouble breathing. I had to unplug my nose. As soon as I released my fingers from my nostrils, the taste of cheese was overwhelming, causing the memory of puking up all the vile-tasting Cheez Whiz to resurface. I tried to swallow, but when I did I began to gag. The food didn't make it all the way down my throat; it was stuck. I tried to swallow harder to force it down, but it wouldn't budge. I tried to cough, but for some reason I couldn't. The food was really stuck, and I began to panic. I stood up and instinctively put my hands over my throat indicating that I was choking. My sisters momentarily stared at me in disbelief. I willed myself to swallow but couldn't. I stuck my hand down my throat and tried to grab the partially chewed-up cheese stick, but it was lodged too deeply. My eyes began to tear up as I gasped for air. I coughed harder, forcing tiny pieces of partially chewed-up cheese stick to go flying across the table at Liz and Charlie. They stared at me stunned and frozen with fear.

Everything around me was starting to go fuzzy, and Liz's voice was muffled as she stood up and frantically screamed, "Help, my sister is choking!" loudly enough for the entire restaurant to hear.

As my body grew limp and I began to fall to the floor, I felt someone quickly wrap his arms around me and prop me upright. "It's okay; I'm a doctor," the man behind me reassured my sisters and me as he began to furiously thrust his fist into my abdomen.

With each thrust of his fist, my body flopped forward and then backwards like a rag doll until finally the thick glob of chewed-up cheese stick went flying out of my mouth. I let out a loud gasp for air, and my lungs eagerly inhaled all the air they could hold. Exhausted, I collapsed into the man's arms, and he laid me flat onto the floor. Once I stopped coughing and gasping for air, my vision went back to normal. I looked up and saw the doctor who had saved me smiling down at me. Beside him stood my frightened aunt Patti and concerned Liz and Charlie. The man shined a light into my eyes.

"Her pupils look fine," he reassured Aunt Patti. "Her throat will be sore for the next couple of days, so make sure everything she eats and drinks is cold. That will help soothe her throat. And young lady," he said looking back down at me, "you're to drink lots of milkshakes and eat ice cream—doctor's orders!" and then he winked at me.

As I stood up, I noticed a large crowd had gathered around my family and me. Strangers began to applaud the doctor. He smiled and waved to the crowd then put his arm around me. My face grew red with embarrassment.

The crowd dispersed, and we went back to our table. As we waited for the waitress to bring me a new milkshake and our main courses, I drew the kind doctor a picture on the back of the kids' menu. Before we left, I walked over to his table, thanked him for saving my life, gave him a big hug, and handed him the picture.

As we drove back to Apple's house, my sisters sat silently in the back seat of the car as I happily slurped my large, cool, and refreshing chocolate shake.

"Mom and Dad are going to kill us," I heard Liz whisper to Charlie.

"Yup," Charlie sighed in agreement.

"Okay, girls," Aunt Patti said as she pulled into Apple's driveway, "remember what we practiced telling your parents."

"Em choked, but a doctor helped her, and now she's perfectly fine," Liz repeated.

I jumped out of the car and raced my sisters into the house. "Mom, Dad!" I called as I entered Apple's house. My voice was a little raspy.

Mom looked perplexed. "Hi, Em!" She gave me a hug as she greeted me. "Did you have a good dinner?" Mom asked.

"I almost died on a cheese stick!" I said at the very moment my sisters entered the house. I pulled away from Mom's hug to sip my milkshake. You would think that with Poppy having just passed I would have been a little more concerned about what I had just experienced; however, at that moment, all I knew was that the doctor had told Aunt Patti to let me drink all the milkshakes and eat all the ice cream I wanted for the next couple of days to help heal my throat. Per the doctor's orders, *I* was to be given milkshakes; he hadn't said anything about Charlie and Liz. I was hoping they wouldn't get any milkshakes and would be forced to watch me savor mine day after day until I felt better.

"What?!" Mom asked, puzzled, as Aunt Patti entered Apple's house.

"Yup." I shrugged my shoulders. "A doctor squeezed my belly, and my food went flying out of my mouth, and my throat hurts," I said as I rubbed my throat.

Mom's eyes filled with tears as she pulled me in tighter.

"Oh, and the doctor said to rest and drink lots of milkshakes," I said as I pushed Mom away and skipped into the back room and hopped into Poppy's blue chair. I reached for the remote and turned on Disney. There was a lot of commotion coming from the front room, but I sat happily in Poppy's chair sipping on my milkshake as I watched *Are You Afraid of the Dark*, a show I wasn't allowed to watch but knew I could get away with watching today.

I will never know the name of the doctor who saved my life that Saturday night at T.G.I. Friday's, but I am eternally grateful. To this day I still don't like canned cheese and am very cautious eating fried cheese. As for Charlie and Liz, they spent the next few days sulking as they watched me enjoy milkshake after milkshake after milkshake.

Speak Now
or Forever Hold Your Pee

It had been a long, hard year of adjusting to being back in all-day preschool and mourning the loss of our amazing Poppy. Not only had my daily routine changed but family celebrations and holidays just weren't the same without Poppy. This year had been particularly hard on Apple, Mom, and my aunts. We were in need of a vacation to somewhere far away from the painful memories that lingered in our hearts and homes. It was time for a dip adventure.

Taking a girls' trip was nothing new to our family; the women in my family often went on weekend getaways together. Most of the time we ventured to Gatlinburg, Tennessee, for a weekend in a cabin. The big trips—such as Florida or South Carolina—were taken after school was out and Mom and Dad had received their income tax return.

Our girls' vacations never seemed to go smoothly; even as a young child I could see that. Like the time our blue minivan packed full of luggage and family decided to die on the highway in the middle of the night. Mom, Apple, my sisters, and I were left stranded in the dark, on the highway, with cars and semi drivers racing past us. This was before cell phones—and no, we didn't have AAA. Or the time when a semi driver didn't see our minivan and began to change lanes. Mom frantically laid on her horn and put the pedal to the metal, forcing the semi back into his own lane. As we passed the truck, Liz thought it would be funny to flip the driver the bird. Needless to say, he did not appreciate Liz's middle-finger gesture.

In return, he decided to speed up until he was next to us then began to intentionally swerve into our lane just enough to push our minivan onto the shoulder. If Mom slowed down, he slowed down; if Mom sped up, he sped up. We were stuck—trapped between the semi and the guardrail—until he decided he had had enough fun. I had never heard Mom cry and scream so many profanities. If only he could have heard her!

It was no wonder Poppy had named our vacations the dip vacations—Mom, my aunts, and Apple being the dips and all the granddaughters being the mini-dips. The car rides themselves were often an adventure of their own.

Mom always offered us souvenir money if we were good on the long ride to our destination. We all started with the same amount of money, but if we fought, Mom would subtract money from our accounts. The better we were, the more money she'd add to our accounts. I always received the most money.

On this particular trip, even before Mom pulled out of the driveway, we girls began to bicker. This was way too soon for us to start fighting, so Mom implemented the quiet game. There were exceptions to the quiet game. You were allowed to speak if Mom or Apple spoke to you, if you were asking for the snack bag, or if you had to tell Mom to stop soon so you could use the restroom. I could play the quiet game for not just hours but through entire states. I had a secret weapon—my thumb!

Yes, I was a thumb-sucker. As long as I had my green blanket and my thumb, I was set. This was the only thing I didn't care if my sisters made fun of me about. I loved my thumb. It didn't matter if my sisters kicked the back of my seat or pulled my hair; I had had a taste of the precious souvenir money. The money Mom gave us we could spend on whatever we wanted—candy, toys, anything! Nothing could break my determination to get the most money.

Twenty minutes into the trip, after we had just crossed the bridge into Kentucky, I had to pee. I had forgotten to use the bathroom before we left the house.

"Mom," I said from the back seat. Immediately both of my sisters looked at me wide-eyed thinking I was the first to lose at the quiet game.

"Yes, Em," she replied from the driver's seat.

"I have to pee," I shamefully said, knowing I had broken one of Mom's cardinal rules: always use the restroom before leaving the house.

"Already, Em?" she asked in a somewhat annoyed voice.

I nodded my head yes.

"Okay," she said letting out a small sigh, knowing the twelve-hour car ride was going to be more like a sixteen-hour or more car ride.

"We'll stop soon," she reassured me, glancing back at me through the rearview mirror.

I stuck my thumb back in my mouth to keep from talking, closed my eyes, snuggled up with my green blanket, and tried to sleep. I must have drifted off because I woke up some time later to Liz and Charlie arguing over the snack bag.

"I'm deducting money from both of your accounts!" frustrated Mom said from the driver's seat.

Charlie looked annoyed as she put on her headphones, pressed play on her Walkman, and crossed her arms over her chest in a huff. Liz just shrugged her shoulders and continued to read her Babysitter's Club book.

I crossed my legs trying to hold in my pee. Mom seemed irritated with Liz and Charlie, so now was not the time to remind her that I still had to pee. I closed my eyes and tried to fall back asleep.

I woke up some time later to Apple and Mom laughing over stories from Mom's childhood, Charlie still listening to her Walkman, Liz still reading, and me now feeling as if my bladder was going to burst at any moment.

"Mom!" I squealed from the back seat as I tightened my legs willing myself not to pee in my pants.

My sisters both looked at me, waiting to see what I had to say since I hadn't spoken in hours.

"Yes, Em?" Mom asked.

"Now I really, really have to pee!" I hollered as tears filled my eyes.

"Oh, my goodness, I'm so sorry, Em. I completely forgot!" Mom said sympathetically as she glanced over at Apple.

"You've been asleep for the entire state of Kentucky, Em!" Apple explained. "We're in Tennessee."

"Humph" I let out an uncomfortable sigh. If winning the quiet game meant peeing in my pants, I'd rather take the deduction from my spending account.

Liz and Charlie smiled and looked at each other. As always, they found pleasure in my discomfort. They gave each other the head nod. No words needed to be exchanged to know how to torture me.

Charlie was the first to taunt me: "Ocean waves crashing into the shore…"

"Dripping water…" Liz smiled at Charlie as she joined in on the fun. "Drip…drip…drip."

"Rushing waterfalls…" Charlie laughed as she leaned closer to me and whispered "Ssshhh" into my ear.

"Ohhh, nnnoooo," I tightened my legs even harder.

"Sisters, sisters, there were never such devoted sisters," Apple began to sing from the front seat. This was the song she'd sing to us whenever we were fighting or picking on one another—her own personal warning indicating that we needed to stop before it was too late and we were in trouble with Mom. As always, Apple was right.

"I'd be careful if I were you two," Mom scorned as she glanced back at Liz and Charlie in the rearview mirror. "If she pees in her pants, the minivan will smell like pee for the rest of the trip! And we still have a long—and I mean a LONG—way to go," Mom lectured.

Liz and Charlie looked at each other, and instantly their attitudes changed from amused to annoyed. Mom had made a good point. Getting a rise out of picking on their little sister was one thing; having the van smell like pee was another.

"How could you make poor little Emily hold her pee for four hours, Mom!?" Liz questioned.

"Yeah, Mom!" Charlie joined Liz in ganging up on Mom. "That's practically child abuse."

"We should report you to 241- KIDS," Liz added.

"Uh-huh," Charlie sassed as she nodded her head in agreement.

"Oh, girls!" Apple shook her head and let out a little laugh.

"Liz," Mom said in a serious voice, "hold up the red sign!" she commanded.

Since we were traveling before the days of cell phones, we used paper signs to signal to our aunts and cousins in the car behind us. We had signs indicating that we needed to stop for gas, food, the restroom, and for an emergency. The red sign meant we needed to stop ASAP. We hadn't used the red sign before. Mom meant business.

Liz worked quickly to hold up the red sign in the rear window, and Mom warned us all to hold on as she hit the accelerator and whipped the minivan into the exit lane causing all of our seat belts to tighten around our chests as we swayed to the left.

Mom was always a cautious driver. She has never had a speeding ticket—or a ticket of any kind for that matter. Liz liked to tease Mom and often called her a grandma driver, especially when Mom drove under the speed limit. Well, not at that moment. Mom was driving more like a racecar driver than a grandma. She was determined to get me to a bathroom before the minivan smelled like pee from Tennessee to South Carolina.

She pulled into the nearest gas station. There was no time to explain the use of the red sign as she frantically pulled into a parking spot and moved faster than I've seen her move before to get the minivan door open and grab me out of my seat.

As soon as I went from sitting to standing, my body registered how full my bladder was. The pressure was unbearable, and I couldn't control what happened next. As I felt the warm liquid go down my leg, I tightened my legs as hard as I could and began to cry. Not only was I embarrassed to be six years old and having an accident but my sisters would find out, and I would never hear the end of it.

Mom was still moving at supermom speed though and somehow got me to the bathroom before I full-on peed in my pants. As I walked out of the bathroom stall, sniffling and hanging my head low, Mom awaited me with a hug.

"I'm so sorry, Em," she said, consoling me, "It was all my fault. Will you please forgive me?" she asked as she worked quickly to wash off my legs with a soapy towel from the bathroom dispenser.

I gave Mom a little head nod but still was too embarrassed to look her in the eye.

"Your sisters won't know," she reassured me as she grabbed dry towels and patted my legs dry. "I have a plan." She threw away the towels and knelt down so she could see my eyes. "When we go back to the car, I'll tell them to get out, stretch their legs, and use the bathroom while I fill up the van with gas. When they're gone, I'll grab you a pair of clean underwear and shorts from your bag, and you can change in the car; they'll never know," she reassured me.

I stood close to Mom and followed her lead. Her plan worked like a charm. When my sisters returned from the restroom, I was already buckled in my seat, covered up with my blanket, and ready to go. As they climbed back into the van, I held my breath waiting for them to make a joke about me smelling like pee, but to my surprise they didn't notice anything.

As soon as we were back on the highway, Liz and Charlie joined forces again to tease Mom about how neglectful she was to her children. At first Mom silently took the abuse, still feeling bad about what had happened; however, as soon as I joined in on the fun, Mom and Apple began to laugh along.

After a while they grew bored of poking fun at Mom and turned to our go-to car ride games: I Spy, Would You Rather, finding license plates from different states, singing along to the music on the radio, and listening to Apple's stories about her childhood. To this day, we still can't believe that when Apple and her sister, Aunt Patrice, were kids, they could buy a cola for just a nickel.

Looking back, I miss the simplicity of our family vacation car rides. Without cell phones, iPads, iPods, or DVD players to occupy our time, we spent the long drives talking—even if it meant my sisters picking on me—listening to and sharing stories, and making up games.

Sharks and Nudists

I've always envied my sisters and their carefree attitude towards the ocean. Charlie is fearless and up for any adventure. She could boogie board the biggest waves and swim and wander aimlessly in the never-ending ocean for hours. As an adult, Charlie is the only one of us McCoy Boys to live by the ocean and enjoy scuba diving.

As for Liz, she has always been indifferent towards the ocean. If Charlie wanted her to join her boogie boarding or exploring, she would, but it was obvious that she didn't enjoy it as much as Charlie did. The older Liz got, the more she came to prefer working on her tan instead of being in the water.

When I was a child, if my sisters weren't right by my side when we were in the ocean, I would be absolutely terrified. Why? Well, I don't like the fact that (a) I can't see what's swimming around me, (b) I can't see what I'm stepping on, and (c) I'm swimming in a shark's home. I am absolutely terrified of sharks! I don't know what this fear stems from, but after this particular family vacation, the fear only intensified.

While on vacation, to help keep my fears at bay, Mom bought me water shoes so I wouldn't have to feel the nastiness of the mushy ocean floor and a special "shark-repellent" bathing suit. This bathing suit was special because, according to Mom, sharks don't like the color pink. My new pink bathing suit made me invincible not only to sharks but to all scary ocean creatures. Thank goodness for the color pink!

We were only a couple of days into our vacation, so my sisters were still including me in the games they were playing. I think it was the excitement of being away from home that filled Liz and Charlie with kindness. They'd always kick off vacation in full-blown sisterly love mode, including me in everything—building sandcastles, jumping ocean waves, and playing Marco Polo and Sharks and Minnows in the pool. As the days passed though, they'd grow tired of including me in their activities. Building sandcastles turned into burying me in the sand only to leave me stuck while they'd run off and go boogie boarding, an activity Mom had deemed too dangerous for me until I was a little bigger. After I'd escape from the sand, I'd sit on the shoreline digging for interesting seashells and watching my sisters ride the waves without me.

This vacation day was a beautiful, warm summer day, and us McCoy Boys were in our bathing suits heading out to jump waves in the ocean. This was the first year Mom had allowed me to go out deeper than my waist. Mom's rules for being in the ocean were simple: don't go deeper than the limit she assigned and stay where she could see us.

One thing I believe all young siblings have in common is that when your older siblings offer to include you in something, even if you're scared and don't want to do it, you suck it up and do whatever they want. Why? Well, for me, the answer was simple: having my sisters want to spend time with me without torturing me happened once in a blue moon and was a dream come true. Those rare moments became some of the best memories from my childhood. Even if I was terrified of the ocean, I thought I was hot stuff to be hanging out with my older (and cooler, as they liked to remind me) sisters. Not to mention, Mom let me go out farther than waist-high when I was with Liz and Charlie, and that made me feel big and brave. So, with my water shoes and shark-repellent pink bathing suit on, I took a big deep breath, wrapped my arms around Charlie's neck, and we began to venture out into the ocean.

Liz, Charlie, and I were having fun bobbing up and down in the waves. Occasionally, when a big wave would come, I'd tighten my grip on Charlie as we'd hold our breath and try to swim through the wave. The waves would give us a rush of excitement as they pushed us back towards the shore. Liz and Charlie were like my personal boogie board. With my sisters by my side and my shark-repellent bathing suit on, for the first time I was able to relax and enjoy the ocean. I was having the time of my life—that is, until my sisters decided to break Mom's rule and swim out farther.

Once I knew Charlie couldn't touch the ocean floor anymore and was now treading water with me on her back, bobbing in the waves, I began to get nervous. Yes, Charlie was the strongest of us girls, but what if she wasn't strong enough to keep us both afloat? I glanced back to see how far we were from the shoreline; Mom looked like a little dot. We were too far out, and I knew my sisters knew it. I began to panic, and to make matters worse, I felt something brush up against my leg, and instant chills went up my leg and spine. I had had enough fun.

"You can take me back now, Charlie," I said, trying not to sound too scared.

"Aw, come on, Em," Charlie said. "Don't worry; I got you!" Charlie was being sincere. She loved the ocean and was having fun. She was trying to be nice and include me in something, so who was I to keep complaining?

However, even with my water shoes and shark-repellent bathing suit on, whatever brushed up against me felt slimy and big. Fear began to replace the excitement of having my sisters include me.

"Come on, guys," Liz hollered over to us. "Some big waves are coming!"

"But I… I felt something on my leg," I said embarrassingly to my sisters.

"It was probably just a fish," Charlie said. "We are in the ocean, Em," she reminded me of the obvious.

"We'll catch the next big wave then head in," Liz said. Liz was always looking out for me.

I nodded and let out a sigh of relief. Her plan seemed reasonable, but I was still nervous. I knew it was most likely just a fish that had brushed up against me, but still I didn't like not being able to see what was below me. I began to scan the ocean around us. The waves were beautiful the way the sunlight reflected off the water. In the distance, to the left of us, I saw something stick out from the beautiful blue waves. Then, as quickly as it had appeared, it disappeared. I swallowed hard. I'm sure I was just imagining things; however, I couldn't help but keep my eyes glued in that direction. A moment later I saw the object reappear, only this time it seemed a little closer, and there wasn't one; there were two—or maybe even three—next to it. My stomach tightened. I knew I wasn't imagining things, and I knew exactly what the objects were.

"Liz!" I cried. "Charlie! Look!" I screamed as I pointed to where I had just spotted several shark fins.

"What is it?" Liz asked.

"I think it's a… a shark," I squealed as my body began to tremble, and I tightened my grip around Charlie's neck.

"Come on, Em," Charlie pleaded, "don't be a scaredy-ca—" Charlie's sentence was interrupted by whistles blowing from the shoreline. I turned my head to see lifeguards rushing into the water frantically blowing their whistles.

"Shark!" I heard people screaming.

"Oh shi—" Liz screamed as she turned around and began to frantically swim towards us and the shore.

"Out of the water!" Another lifeguard was screaming as Charlie quickly turned around.

I tightened my grip around Charlie and held my breath as she began to swim faster than she had ever swum before. I was scared and was having trouble holding my breath. I kept having to tap Charlie's shoulder, my cue for her to come up so I could get air. I knew Charlie was swimming as fast as she could with me on her back, but I was worried that we weren't swimming quickly enough. If I tried to kick my legs to help her, we'd just end up kicking each other. It was counterproductive, so I just continued to hold on.

"Come on, Em," Charlie said when we were up for air. "Big breath in!" she hollered right before going under again.

Liz was in front of us, getting closer to the shore, but it seemed Charlie and I were farther out than anyone else. I could just picture

Mom frantically running into the ocean to try to get to us. Little did I know, the lifeguards weren't allowing anyone to enter the water. In the chaos of people racing to the shoreline from every direction and knowing there were sharks nearby, I was having trouble concentrating on holding my breath.

As Charlie swam as fast as she could, I tapped her shoulder again indicating that I needed to come up for air, but she didn't come up. So I tapped a little harder this time as my lungs began to beg for air; Charlie still didn't come up. I couldn't hold my breath any longer; I had to let go of Charlie. My lungs were burning, begging for air.

When I surfaced, I quickly gasped for air only to have a little splash of ocean water enter my mouth. I began to gag on the water just in time for a wave to come crashing down on me. The wave sent me back underwater before I had time to take a breath. I was in full-blown panic mode now as I willed myself to resurface so I could breathe. The harder I tried, the farther the distance felt between my face and the water's surface. At this point, I was sure I was going to pass out in the ocean. Knowing sharks were hot on my trail, all I could think was that sharks don't like the color pink—my saving grace.

I really don't think my sisters meant to leave me alone in the shark-infested waters; however, if it weren't for the lifeguards working that day, I could easily have been left for shark bait. Suddenly I felt someone yank me out from under the water in one swift motion. The next thing I knew, I was coughing so hard that it made me puke up the ocean water I had swallowed. I opened my eyes to see a guy I had never seen before holding me in his muscular arms. The lifeguard worked fast to get me back to the shore. Hysterical, Mom, Liz, and Charlie were all awaiting my safe return. When the lifeguard put me down, I ran to Mom and gave her a big hug. I had never been so scared.

"Thank you, thank you," Mom said to the lifeguard as she held me tight, "I was so worried about her." Mom was crying now as she picked me up and held me on her hip.

"It's okay, Mom." I hugged her hard. "I have my shark-repellent swimsuit on!" I said trying to reassure her. Yes, I had been scared, but I wasn't used to seeing Mom so upset, and I wanted to comfort her.

"Just doing my job, ma'am," the lifeguard, a little out of breath, said to Mom, and then he looked at me. "You need to be careful in the ocean, sweetie. There's no such thing as a shark-repellent swimsuit." He patted me on the head and turned to leave.

As I watched the lifeguard run off, I tried to process what he had just said to me. A sickening feeling came over me as I realized that Mom had lied to me! *There was no such thing as a shark-repellent bathing suit?!* And not only had Mom lied to me but my sisters had left me unprotected in shark-infested waters. I was pissed. I should have peed in the van!

I pushed myself out of Mom's grip. Once I was free from the liar's arms, I stood directly in front of her, put my hands on my hips, and stared her dead in the eyes, then I looked at Liz, and then at Charlie. If looks could kill, the lifeguard would have raced back to do CPR on all three of them.

"I was just trying to help you have a fun vacation, Em." Mom bent down on her knees so her face would be closer to mine. She looked sorry, but at the moment I was too mad and hurt to care. I didn't know what to say; I had never been this upset with her until now.

I turned my attention to my sisters, both looking very guilty, but again I was too mad to care. I didn't bother letting them explain themselves.

"I want to un-sister you!" I shouted as I looked deep into Charlie's eyes and then added, "Both of you!" as I looked at Liz.

They looked stunned. After all, I was their little sister who idolized them.

I crossed my arms angrily across my chest as I turned and stomped my little feet in the sand all the way over to our beach chairs. There I sat, next to Apple, sulking and not saying a word as angry tears streamed down my face.

I looked over to my sisters and watched as they hung their heads low in shame, and Mom shook her angry finger at them. It had been their job to protect me, and they had failed miserably. After Mom was finished, they all walked over to the beach chairs to join Apple and me.

Charlie, Liz, and I sat in silence as we watched a team of people work with a boat and huge nets to get the sharks away from the shoreline. I kept my eyes glued on the workers. I refused to even glance in my sisters' direction.

After the lifeguards gave the okay to go back into the water, Liz and Charlie went back in but no farther than their waist. Mom had instituted the waist-high rule for the rest of vacation. Charlie was clearly heartbroken not to have free range over the ocean. I watched with a sinister smile on my face, secretly happy that some of her joy had been taken away. Ah, sisterly love!

That night Mom let me pick where we went for dinner. Since I wasn't talking to Mom, Liz, or Charlie, I told Apple that I wanted to go to Barefoot Landing, and she relayed the message to Mom. We all piled in the car and headed to the local shopping complex.

Whenever we visited Myrtle Beach, I always loved going to Barefoot Landing. It had it all—arcades, stores, restaurants, ice cream shops. One of my favorite memories from Barefoot Landing—besides the crazy pigeon that attacked Aunt Patti and then pooped in her hair— was riding the carousel at night. I loved the way the lights reflected off the water and the feeling of the cool, salty night breeze rushing through my hair. Oh, the simple pleasures of youth!

Before riding the carousel we'd eat dinner at one of the restaurants on the strip and then hit up the arcade. Us McCoy Boys could spend hours in an arcade. Although I can't remember the name of the arcade, there was a game there that I will never forget—Feed Big Bertha. I'm just going to repeat that one more time—Feed Big Bertha. I mean, really? Offensive? Yes. Hilarious to a child? Absolutely. The game was a giant head of a lady with a huge, oversized mouth and crazy red hair. After giving the machine your money, Bertha's face would light up, and a lady's voice would say, "Feed me; I'm hungry." Balls would then come down a chute, and you would try to throw them into the giant lady's mouth. If you got a ball to go in her mouth, she'd say things like "Yum, more!" as her parachute-inflatable body would grow bigger and bigger the more balls you threw into her mouth. If you missed her mouth, Big Bertha would taunt you with sayings such as "I'm hungry" and "Come on, feed me!" I don't remember the purpose of the game or how you could beat it, but this strange game never failed to amuse my sisters and me.

* * *

The next day of vacation, I was still mad at Mom for lying about the shark-repellent bathing suit and my sisters for abandoning me in the ocean with sharks hot on our trail. I was determined to spend the day avoiding my sisters.

After my daily morning walk on the beach with Apple, I headed over to the area of the beach where my sisters were swimming only to turn my back to them so I couldn't see them playing in the shallow ocean water. There I sat by myself trying to have fun building a sand castle, but I couldn't help but wish Cousin Jon had come along with us on this vacation. On last year's vacation, he was caught running around the pool area peeing on all the geckos. His little peeing adventure got us McCoy Boys banned from the pool the last couple of days of vacation. Needless to say, he wasn't invited back this year.

For the finishing touch to my sandcastle, I added a moat around it to keep my sisters out. All I needed now was water for my moat. I picked up my bucket to go fill it up with water, and that's when he appeared. A boy with dark, curly hair, golden skin, and dark eyes was standing next to me. He was wearing a Speedo, orange water wings, a gold chain around his neck, and carrying a bag of strawberries. He didn't say anything. He just smiled and waved and popped a strawberry in his mouth. He was over a head taller than me, but that was nothing new. (Even as an adult, I only stand at a towering four feet, eight inches.)

I smiled, waved back, and then walked my bucket to the ocean, filled it with water, and came back to my fort. I was surprised to see the boy still standing there when I returned. I poured the water into the moat and headed to the ocean to refill my pail. The boy continued to watch me and eat his strawberries as I worked. The moat was deep and needed a lot of water. After I had filled and dumped my pail about ten times, I sat down to take a little break. When I sat down, the boy picked up my pail, handed me his bag of strawberries, and went to work filling my pail with water and dumping it into my moat.

It was now mid-day and getting hotter by the minute. After about the fifth time of filling my pail, the boy set it down and wiped the sweat off his forehead. That's when it happened—something simply unforgettable. Standing right in front of me, the boy bent over, lowered his Speedo, and then proceeded to step out of them. The boy was completely naked!

I gasped in horror as I quickly covered my eyes with my hands trying to erase the image of his boy parts literally right in front of my face. I didn't see that one coming! The boy didn't even seem fazed to be standing naked on a beach surrounded by strangers. He began to speak a language that I didn't understand as he grabbed my hand and pulled me up from the ground. He was stronger than me, and it didn't take much time for him to have me off the ground. Although he had managed to pry my hands from my face, I kept my eyes tightly closed as the boy dragged me alongside him.

Once I felt the cool water on my feet, I couldn't help but open my eyes. After all, I needed to stay safe. The boy was smiling and laughing as he splashed and kicked water up at me. And yes, he was still naked. I looked towards Mom willing her to come rescue me. In the distance I saw her and Apple lounging in their beach chairs. It was no use; they weren't looking in my direction.

The boy was oblivious that I was uncomfortable with his nakedness. I stood frozen in place not knowing what to do.

Immediately I thought of Charlie and Liz but then reminded myself that I had un-sistered them. Between the sharks and my new nude friend, I couldn't help but feel as if this vacation was all a bad dream.

Then out of nowhere a woman in a very small bikini that hardly covered her private parts came screaming at the boy. Although I didn't speak their language, I knew the woman was my nude friend's mom and that he was in trouble. She was holding his swim trunks in one hand and shaking her finger at him with the other. She forced him to put his Speedo back on. While he was getting dressed, Charlie and Liz ran up behind me laughing hysterically.

"Who's your new naked friend, Em?" Charlie asked in between laughs.

Liz was laughing so hard she was bent over at the waist holding her stomach. Despite how mad I was at my sisters, seeing them laugh so hard, I couldn't help but smirk back at them. I wasn't ready to forgive my sisters or spend time with them, but I was amused with their interest in my friend. It was obvious the boy didn't speak English and wasn't going to tell us his name, so I gave him the name Strawberry.

After Strawberry put his Speedo back on, we spent the rest of the day playing in the ocean and building sandcastles together. When it was time to head in for the night, Strawberry gave me a big hug and a kiss on the cheek. I was shocked. No boy besides Dad or Poppy had ever kissed me. My face was bright red with embarrassment. Mom explained to me that Strawberry was European, and they do things a little differently than we do here in the US.

That night as we all walked back to our room, my sisters came up with a little song to tease me with. They sang:

Strawberry, Strawberry, Emily's man,
Tried to pick her up without a plan.
He worked all day in his water wings,
Sometime he'd call her, a-ring-a-ding-ding.

My sisters were always clever when it came to teasing me. That wasn't the last time I'd see Strawberry or hear that song. His family was staying at the same hotel as we were. For the remainder of our stay, we'd run into Strawberry in the pool and on the beach. Every time I'd see him, he was in a Speedo and orange water wings. And yes, whenever he'd get too hot, he'd strip down naked only to have his Mom yell at him and force him to get dressed.

Although this vacation was traumatizing in more ways than one, I will never forget almost being eaten by sharks and being pursued by my first boyfriend, Strawberry. Although I had un-sistered Charlie and Liz on that vacation, that trip to Myrtle Beach was one of my favorite family vacations.

Several years later, us McCoy Boys would return to Myrtle Beach. That year, my sisters gave me a new nickname—Emmie the Hemi. According to my sisters, just like a hemorrhoid, I was a pain in their butts. One night when we went to Barefoot Landing to visit Big Bertha and eat dinner, we happened to wander into a shop with metal signs hanging all over the walls. My sisters laughed as they spotted the perfect sign to hang in my room: 426 Hemi Road. They eagerly chipped in what was left of their vacation spending money to buy the Hemi sign for me as a birthday present. As a child, this would be the only present I would ever receive from Charlie and Liz that they had bought with their own money.

Once we returned home, Mom proudly hung the sign on my bedroom wall, impressed that Charlie and Liz had used their vacation money to buy me a present. Mom actually thought they were innocently rhyming Emmie with Hemi. Cute, right? Wrong! Little did Mom know, nothing Liz and Charlie did for me was ever sweet or innocent. I knew Hemi was a reference to Charlie and Liz's personal hemorrhoid.

Cry-Baby

For a seven-year-old there was no better way to spend a Friday night than with all my girl cousins at Apple Betty's house watching movies. Sure, my sisters were there too, but Liz had Margo to hang out with, Charlie had Penny, and I had Lynn and Lauren. During these movie nights, my sisters were preoccupied, making torturing me low on their priority list.

Not only did Apple let us drink pop, eat snacks, and stay up as late as we wanted but also she'd let us be as loud as we wanted. Before watching movies, we'd collaborate to make up skits and dance routines and after we'd perfected them, Apple would let us use her coffee table as our stage while we'd take turns performing. Apple would applaud and judge us on our performances. She was the coolest grandma!

After our show was over, the seven of us would open up our sleeping bags on the living room floor then we'd gather in the kitchen to grab all our snacks and drinks. Once we had our popcorn and soda, we'd settle in for a movie. Throughout the years, our girl movie nights were spent watching mostly classics such as *Gone with the Wind*, *The Sound of Music*, *Seven Brides for Seven Brothers*, and *The Wizard of Oz*.

This year, Liz and Margo were outgrowing movie nights with their younger sisters and cousins. After we finished the first VHS of *The Sound of Music*, Apple said goodnight and headed to her room. Instead of putting in the second VHS to finish the movie, Margo jumped up, made her way to her bag, and pulled out a VHS I hadn't seen before. On the front cover of the movie box was a girl wearing tight pink pants and a pink top. Next to the pretty girl was a good-looking guy dressed in black with a single tear running down his cheek. The title read *Cry-Baby*, a name Liz and Charlie often called me.

"Aren't you guys getting sick of watching the same old movies over and over?" Margo asked.

"Um, yeah," Liz eagerly agreed as she sat up from her sleeping bag to get a better look at what Margo had in her hand.

I was five years younger than Margo, and I thought she was the coolest person on earth. She was the prettiest girl I knew. Her hair was always perfect, she was allowed to wear makeup, and she was a cheerleader. As a spoiled only child, her mother bought her all the newest fashions. Talk about a cool older cousin; I wanted to be just like her!

Honestly, I didn't care what we watched; I was just happy to be watching a movie with my cousins and eating junk food—and I was grateful that Liz and Charlie weren't ganging up on me.

"Whatcha got there?" Charlie asked Margo as we all watched her take the VHS out of its case and pop it into the VCR.

"A movie I think you'll like," Margo said grinning ear to ear. "But we can only watch it if no one," she stressed, "and I mean no one," she added looking at Lauren and me, "tells her parents!"

Liz and Charlie immediately turned their heads towards me.

"What?!" I asked somewhat confused. I might have been the youngest, but I knew better than to tattle on Charlie and Liz.

"Why aren't we allowed to tell our parents?" Lauren, who was my age, asked confused.

"Because it's rated PG-13," Margo said with a mischievous grin.

PG-13?! I gasped to myself. Back then, watching a PG-13 movie before you were thirteen was unheard of.

"How'd you get it?" I asked. Although Margo had just turned twelve, I knew my aunt and uncle, and there was no way they would have let her watch a PG-13 movie.

Margo shrugged her shoulders and said, "From a friend," as she pressed play.

Penny and Charlie excitedly sat up and moved their sleeping bags closer to the TV. Breaking the rules was nothing new to either one of them. I could just hear Charlie bragging to her friends Monday at school. "What'd I do this weekend?" she'd say coolly to her friends. "Oh you know—watched a PG-13 movie, but nothing too exciting." She'd grin as all her friends turn green with envy.

Lynn, Lauren, and I just looked at one another. We knew that if we tattled to Apple, everyone would hate us, and that would be the end of girl cousins movie nights; however, we didn't like to disobey our parents. We were in a tough spot.

"Do what you want," I said, "I'm going to bed," and I lay down in my sleeping bag.

"Us too," Lauren and Lynn agreed as they lay down next to me.

As the movie played, curiosity got the better of me. I couldn't help but want to watch so I could see what a PG-13 movie was all about. To my surprise, there was music and singing in the movie, which made it even more appealing. (A little background: The movie *Cry-Baby* takes place in the 1950s. Bad boy Cry-Baby Walker, a "drape," falls in love with good girl Allison, a "square," and their love story unfolds. This movie has it all: teenage pregnancy, fights, make-out scenes, bad language, and even scenes in juvenile detention. Bottom line —the movie is completely inappropriate for a seven-year-old.)

While we watched the movie, I couldn't help feeling torn inside. The more I watched, the more I realized I shouldn't be watching, and realizing I shouldn't be watching while everyone around me was enjoying it made me want to watch it even more. My eyes were glued to the TV.

That night, we didn't sleep. We replayed that inappropriate PG-13 movie over and over until the break of dawn. When morning came, we had memorized lines, songs, and dance routines.

Later that week, while playing with my Fisher-Price dollhouse, I renamed all my dolls and gave them new names from *Cry-Baby*.

My favorite dolls— my twin dolls—were now Susie-Q and Snare Drum. The pregnant doll was now Pepper, and the mom and dad dolls were Allison and Cry-Baby. As for the doll that Liz and Charlie had colored all over the face and ruined—it now had the name of Hatchet-Face. I even had a creepy-looking old doll that was none other than Uncle Belvedere Rickettes.

I used my dolls to role-play my favorite parts from *Cry-Baby*. On this particular evening, while I thought I was alone in the family room, Mom had taken a break from cleaning and folding laundry. As I sat on the floor playing with my dolls and dollhouse, my back was turned to Mom, who was leaning in the doorway watching her youngest, sweetest daughter play. That night my role-play went a little something like this....

Allison to Cry-Baby: "I don't know if I'll fit in here."

Cry-Baby: "You're cool—just square, Allison"

Hatchet-Face doll talking to Allison: "You got breasts (except I didn't use the word "breasts"; I used the slang word for "breast" that starts with the letter "t"); stick them out!"

Pepper to Allison: "If you're gonna be Cry-Baby's girl, you gotta learn that our bazooms are our weapons!"

Hatchet-Face to Pepper: "Allison needs a bad-girl makeover."

The girl dolls go into the bedroom where they pretend to do the Allison doll's hair and make-up then come back downstairs to Cry-Baby.

Cry-Baby to Allison: "You look so good painted up like trash! Kiss me hard, Allison!"

Allison to Cry-Baby: "But Cry-Baby, I've never French kissed before."

Cry-Baby: "It feels real good. You open your mouth, I open mine, and we let our tongues wiggle. It's real sexy."

Then I made my dolls kiss, making kissing noises like the ones I heard in the movie. After they were done kissing, they walked over to Uncle Belvedere Rickettes, who was in the bathtub.

Uncle Belvedere Rickettes: "Woo-wee, you caught me in my birthday suit—buck naked!"

Cry-Baby to Uncle Belvedere Rickettes: "We're going to the Jukebox Jamboree."

Uncle Belvedere Rickettes: "Well, take your knocked-up sister."

Cry-Baby, Allison, pregnant teenager Pepper, and Hatchet-Face all leave the house and head to the Jukebox Jamboree next door. They are all dancing when another lady doll comes dancing up to Cry-Baby.

"Cry-Baby," she says "I'm pregnant with your baby."

Pepper: "No you ain't, Lenora. My brother wouldn't touch your breasts (except I used the inappropriate "t" word again) with a ten-foot pole!"

And then all my girl dolls start fighting and smacking one another. End scene.

This is about the time Mom stepped in and interrupted my role-playing. You can imagine Mom's horror and disappointment. She had just witnessed her seven-year-old use inappropriate language and sexual innuendos and make her girl dolls fight over a boy—all things that I shouldn't know anything about.

After a quick phone call to Margo's house, Liz and Charlie were called downstairs where we were given a very firm talking-to. My dolls and dollhouse were taken away for a long time. When they were given back, I had new rules to follow: no more letting my dolls do inappropriate things or use inappropriate language. I wasn't allowed to quote *Cry-Baby*, and I had to give all my dolls more "normal, non-*Cry-Baby*" names. Needless to say, from that day on, our sleepovers were never the same. Movies were monitored, and bedtimes were assigned. Never again would we have as much fun as we had on *Cry-Baby* movie night.

Coney Island

A year had come and gone, and good old summertime had rolled around again. Every June, my parents attended a huge party to celebrate Mom's brother's and close friend's birthdays. They rented out a lodge at a local park and had a celebration fit for royalty—good food, beverages, and even a band. Every year, Apple watched us while my parents had a night out with no kids to worry about and no curfew.

This year their big party just happened to fall on the same day as Mom's company picnic at our local pool and theme park, Coney Island. Coney Island had something for every age—games, roller coasters, and a huge swimming pool. Mom and Dad couldn't pass up anything that was free for us girls, so they decided to take us to the company picnic in the afternoon then head to their party afterwards.

We were excited to attend Mom's company picnic—unlimited food, free ride tickets, and a pool three times bigger than our local pool! Summertime in Cincinnati was hot, and the best way to cool off was to go swimming. Not only was Coney Island's pool bigger than ours but it had a huge, high, metal slide! Our pool only had a diving board. It was especially warm that day, so we decided to start in the pool then ride the rides. That way when we rode the rides, our hair would still be wet, and it would keep us cooled off. We eagerly picked out lounge chairs, threw our towels down, then headed straight for the pool.

This year's trip to Coney Island was special because this was the first company picnic that overly protective Mom and Dad had decided I could swim in the pool without wearing water rings! Not to mention, I was finally tall enough to go down the big metal slide! I was living one of my childhood dreams—free food, free rides, and I was going to conquer my fear of going down the slide.

I followed Liz and Charlie towards the slide and eagerly waited in line. This was it—the day had finally arrived! After years of watching Liz and Charlie go down the slide, I was finally going to go down it too! Our neighborhood diving board was nothing compared to this slide. This slide was huge! You had to walk up what looked like a mile of stairs! (Looking back, it was most likely twelve steps, but at the time it seemed so high.) Once we were at the top, I looked towards Mom and Dad. They looked small and so far away.

"Okay, Em," Liz said as she sat down at the top of the slide. "Watch Charlie and me, and then do as we do, okay?" she instructed as she leaned back. I nodded my head yes and watched as she flew down the slide. The slide flung her off to the side. She disappeared underwater only to resurface a moment later then swim off to the blue rope that roped off the path of the water slide. Mom had instructed her and Charlie to swim off to the side and wait for me.

I stood there on the slide's platform and watched Charlie sit down in front of me, lean back, and put her hands behind her head as she said, "See you at the bottom, loser," as she cruised smoothly down the slide. She hit the water with a small splash, went under, and then resurfaced. She looked up at me, gave me a thumbs-up, and swam over towards Liz.

Although I was excited, I was more than a little nervous. It had taken me weeks to master the diving board at our pool, and I only had a few hours to master my first water slide. The lifeguard standing on the platform could tell I was nervous. He gave me a pat on the back and told me it was my turn. I gulped as I looked down at my sisters who were hanging over the blue rope. They seemed so small. I realized just how high up I was and suddenly wished I had my water rings on for a sense of security. I wanted to go down as coolly as my sisters had, but I couldn't help my knees from wobbling and couldn't take my eyes off the water, which seemed so far away. As I slowly approached the top of the slide, I lost control of my legs. They gave out from under me and I slipped. My bottom hit the hard metal slide with a loud and painful thud, and before I could control any of my own movements, I was flying down the water slide screaming at the top of my lungs.

Instead of cruising smoothly down the slide as I had watched my sisters do, I was flip-flopping from side to side like a fish out of water all the way down the slide. This year I may have met the slide's height requirement, but my weight has always been at least a year behind my age. At my yearly doctor's check-ups, my parents were never surprised to hear that I wasn't on the growth charts—not even in the bottom five percent. I was a tiny little thing, and the water slide knew it. It flung me around like a rag doll.

As I reached the bottom of the slide, I couldn't stop my body from flipping over onto my stomach. As I flew off the slide face down, my forehead smacked against the bottom edge of the slide causing me to instantly blackout. I entered the water floating face down in a small pool of my own blood.

In all the years that Charlie and Liz spent picking on me, they must have been reserving all their true sisterly love for this precise moment. By the way I was flailing and screaming down the slide Charlie and Liz knew something was going terribly wrong. As they swam over to me, some insane, sisterly, overly protective adrenaline must have overtaken them because they beat the lifeguards to my rescue. Charlie was the first one to reach me. She had started to swim from the blue rope to the bottom of the slide as soon as I slipped at the top. She ignored the lifeguard perched at the bottom of the slide—the one furiously blowing her whistle at her telling her to stay outside of the slide's roped-off area. Liz was a close second. She too had been concerned with my screaming, and she too ignored the lifeguard who was yelling at her from the top of the slide. Liz held up a certain finger and quickly swam behind Charlie to my rescue.

They carefully turned my body around, and although they didn't know the correct way to do CPR, Liz supported my back and neck with her arms while Charlie forcefully blew air into my mouth and pounded as hard as she could on my chest. Multiple lifeguards began to show up on the scene as Charlie gave me one more swift, powerful smack in my chest, and I began to forcefully cough up water and gasp for air.

A male lifeguard grabbed me from my sisters' arms and carried me to the side of the pool where my parents anxiously dashed to my side. I continued to cough as Mom cried and Dad hugged me.

Once Charlie and Liz joined us, my family and I were taken to an office where the medical staff examined me. The cut on my forehead wasn't too deep, but they thought I might need stitches. Also, I needed to be watched closely for any signs of a concussion. They recommended my parents take me to Children's Hospital to be evaluated. After a staff member bandaged my forehead, we gathered our belongings and headed to the car.

To my surprise, neither Charlie nor Liz complained about having to leave the amusement park before they had the chance to swim or to use their ride tickets, but I knew they had to be annoyed with me—their little sister who had ruined everything. We had been at the amusement park for only ten minutes when my little accident happened. I was silent on the car ride to the hospital. My head was throbbing from my cut, and my chest hurt from inhaling so much water. Also, I felt awful that I had ruined my family's free day at Coney Island and was worried that I had ruined Mom and Dad's date night too.

Dad, Liz, and Charlie headed to the hospital's cafeteria while Mom stayed with me in the emergency room. After being poked and imaged, I was relieved that I didn't need stitches; however, I did have a minor concussion. The doctors told Mom to keep a close eye on me and to not let me sleep. Mom smiled at me, gave me a loving hug, and told me we'd have a slumber party in the living room and stay up all night watching our favorite movies.

In the car on the way home from the hospital, Mom praised Liz and Charlie for their bravery and love and thanked them for looking out for me. Until this moment I had been in a complete daze from pain. I had never had a headache that bad before. I heard my family talking, but nothing they said really registered. But something inside my mind perked up when I heard the words "looking out for me" and my "sisters" in the same sentence. I made an effort to focus on their conversation. I didn't know what Mom meant when she said they looked out for me.

"What do you mean?" I asked Mom.

"Your sisters beat the lifeguards to your rescue, Em," Mom said with proud tears in her eyes.

"What?" I asked. I remembered the lifeguard holding me and giving me to Mom and Dad, but Charlie and Liz hadn't been anywhere around.

"It's true, Em," Dad said, "They swam over to the bottom of the slide while you were going down."

"They even started CPR on you before the lifeguards arrived," Mom smiled proudly.

"Liz and Charlie rescued me?" I broke this sentence down and slowly processed it in my head. It didn't seem right. They were the ones who were normally hurting me, not saving me! I looked over at Charlie and then at Liz. They were both nonchalantly sipping on their sodas and snacking on the candy Dad had bought them from the hospital's cafeteria. Charlie just shrugged as if it was no big deal, and Liz gave me a loving smile.

Here I thought my family was upset with me for ruining their free day at Coney Island when really my sisters were concerned about me. For once in my life, my sisters did something out of love and concern. They knew when I was going down that slide that I was in trouble, and they came to my rescue. With this realization I began to cry.

"Em, are you okay? Is something wrong? Do we need to go back to the hospital?" Mom frantically asked.

I just sniffled and shook my head no. I was used to my sisters always picking on me, and for the first time, today they protected me. I was crying because I felt loved.

"Quit your crying!" Charlie snapped.

"Yeah, Em," Liz joined in as she playfully laughed.

"You can be such a cry-baby sometimes," Charlie said as she smiled at me.

"Yeah, it's not like you almost died today or anything," Liz teased. And with that my entire family broke into a sad chuckle. We all realized how lucky we had been that day.

"I think Em was a cat in a past life," Charlie said as we all continued to laugh.

"For real," Liz said, "She survived choking on the cheese stick."

"And then there were the sharks," Charlie added.

"And now the infamous Coney Island slide," Liz concluded.

"We're very lucky," Mom added from the front seat. Dad was unusually silent, but his eyes were screaming with concern as he thought about what could have happened to his youngest daughter. At a loss for words, he nodded his head in agreement with Mom.

For the remainder of the car ride home, my sisters teased me about what was left of my nine lives. They were convinced that at the rate I was going, I wouldn't make it out of high school. Leave it to Charlie and Liz to turn a loving situation into a debate about when my nine lives would come to a violent end.

That night, Mom and Dad missed their big party, but the McCoy family had a party of our own. We stayed up late binging on Disney movies and eating pizza and popcorn. Mom and Dad even let us drink real Coke, not the watered-down cokey water they normally tried to give us. Within a few days my headache subsided, and the burning in the back of my throat from coughing up all the chlorine water went away. The cut on my forehead healed nicely, and I was as good as new. As soon as my sisters knew I was back to my normal self, they wasted no time going back to picking on me.

To this day I haven't gone back to Coney Island pool, and I might still have a slight fear of water slides.

A Man and His Boat

Dad grew up the oldest of five kids in Mount Healthy, Ohio. He was never given anything in life. Everything he owned he had worked for—no shortcuts, no breaks. His first job was a paper route at the tender age of eight; however, even at a young age, he didn't spend his hard-earned money on toys or personal pleasure. No, the money he earned was used to help pay bills and to raise his brothers and sisters. Owning a boat had always been a dream of Dad's, and after years of saving, his dream became reality.

Our boat may have been pre-owned and modest, but we didn't care; it was ours, and for the first time, the McCoys were living large. Mom and Dad couldn't afford the slip fee to keep *Blue Beauty*, as we called her, docked at Lake Cumberland, so we kept her parked in our backyard. Hillbilly? Yes. Did we care? Nope. Did the neighbors care? Maybe.

Our neighbor, Mr. Meyer, would watch Dad through the hedges and mumble loudly enough for us all to hear: "I've never seen a man spend so much time on a boat on dry land before. Why not get it on the lake and out of the yard?!" he would protest. What Mr. Meyer said all those years ago holds true to this day: I've never seen a man spend so much time on a boat on dry land as Dad did and still does. Mr. Meyer would never understand just how much Dad loved his new boat.

The first day Dad brought the boat home, he backed her into the backyard, quickly changed into his Hawaiian print shirt and swim trunks, then eagerly began working on the boat. The whole family was excited to welcome *Blue Beauty*. Charlie and I stopped our intense water balloon war and sat down next to Liz, who was sunbathing, and watched Dad. He ordered us to stay off the boat until he had thoroughly inspected her and deemed her safe. We were smart girls. We knew this was Dad-code meaning he wanted time alone on his boat without us girls pestering him.

Dad cranked up Jimmy Buffett on his boom box and washed and polished his newest "baby girl." Since she was brand-new to us, her first wash wasn't good enough, so Dad left Jimmy on re-play while he washed her for the second time and daydreamed of being on the lake. (I think *Blue Beauty* was cleaner than I was that summer.)

After washing her, Dad sorted through all his fishing gear to make sure his tackle box was fully equipped then he washed the life vests he'd purchased at a garage sale for a bargain price and hung them on the clothesline to dry. Finally, he blew up our new lake torpedo to make sure it was big enough for the three of us to fit on. By this time our patience had expired. We had watched long enough without touching a single thing. Excitedly we all plopped down on the plastic torpedo and pretended to ride it.

"Take us to the lake!" Charlie shouted.

"When can we go, Dad?" Liz asked.

"Let's go now!" I insisted.

"Okay, okay, I know you girls are excited, but you can't bounce around on the torpedo when it's on the grass, or you could poke a hole in it—so everyone off!"

We sulked as we sat on the grass next to the torpedo and waited to see what Dad would do next. After watching him inspect the boat and check his supplies for the umpteenth time (it's no wonder my sisters and I all have OCD tendencies), we grew impatient and turned our attention to water wars and pestering one another. Only after Dad had thoroughly completed his prep list did he then kick back in his captain's chair, drink a cold beer, and smoke a cigar while he watched us run wild. This would become Dad's daily routine. While we wreaked havoc in the backyard, he would listen to Jimmy Buffett and daydream about the lake while finishing all his boat prep work.

Our first trip to Lake Cumberland was a typical, crazy-fun McCoy outing. For starters, Mom almost lost *Blue Beauty* as she reversed the van and *Beauty* down the loading dock. Once we were unloaded and successfully on the water, it was our own little slice of heaven. This was the first year Liz was really into sunbathing, so she laid out on one of the side benches while Charlie helped Dad steer the boat. Mom and I sat on the other bench smiling as the wind blew through our hair. The sun was shining, the sky was blue, the weather was warm, but the wind made it perfectly cool. The McCoys were in paradise. We cruised the lake until Charlie grew impatient. She wanted to be the first to test the torpedo.

Dad pulled the boat into a cove and put the torpedo in the water. Mom and Dad worked together to hold it close to the back of the boat while Charlie eagerly got on. They gave her a push and let the water do the rest. Once she was a safe distance behind us, Dad started up the engine and slowly began to pull away, giving Charlie a chance to adjust to the waves bouncing her up and down. Within minutes of being on the torpedo, Charlie was giving us the thumbs-up indicating she wanted to go faster.

Dad sped up *Blue Beauty* and started doing circles to create better waves for Charlie. The torpedo began to rock from side to side, and Charlie had to really hold on. Just when she was getting the hang of the rocking motion, Dad threw the boat into full speed and straightened the wheel. The rope tightened between the torpedo and the boat and whipped Charlie forward. She lost her grip on the rope and went flying off the torpedo doing a cartwheel through the air. Liz and I both laughed as Dad circled around to pick her up.

"That was rad!" she beamed from ear to ear. "Again!"

We all took turns on the torpedo, and by mid-afternoon we considered ourselves professional lake torpedo riders. At one point, all three of us rode the torpedo together. Even though I was stuck riding in between Liz and Charlie, I was having too much fun to care. While we rode, we'd sing songs we'd all memorized from our days spent with Apple:

Keep your mind on the driving,
Keep your hands on the wheel,
Keep your snoopy eyes on the road ahead,
We're having fun kissing and a-hugging,
Kissing and a-hugging with Fred.

When mid-day came, Dad found a quiet, shady cover and threw down the anchor. As Mom and Dad unpacked the cooler and prepared lunch, my sisters and I put on our swim vests and jumped into the cool lake water. While we swam around the boat, Liz and Charlie began to tease me.

"Watch out for the huge lake snakes, Em," Liz warned me.

"They love to nibble on little girls' feet," Charlie chimed in as she swam past me and brushed her leg against my foot.

"Stop it, Charlie!" I screamed as I kicked my feet to make sure it was only Charlie touching me and nothing more. This was our first time on the lake, and I wasn't going to let my sisters ruin the fun.

Charlie and Liz laughed at me.

"For real, Em, there are snakes everywhere in the lake." Liz said.

"So just be careful since you don't have a pink snake-repellent swimsuit," Charlie said as she winked at me.

Instantly the memories of my family lying to me about my shark-repellant bathing suit resurfaced, and not only was I annoyed with my sisters but also became suddenly paranoid of what creatures were swimming beneath me. As Charlie and Liz partook in a water noodle war, I skimmed the water to see if I could see anything swimming around me. Until my sisters mentioned lake snakes, I had assumed the lake was full of fish but nothing scary, but now I pouted as I quickly swam back to the boat and climbed the ladder. I dried off and sat down to eat my salami and pepperoni roll-ups and watched Liz and Charlie play happily in the water without me.

Leave it to my sisters to go and ruin my perfectly good time—story of my life.

After Liz and Charlie had their fill of swimming and had finished eating lunch, Dad taught us how to fish. We spent hours casting our lines and watching our bobbers bob around in the water. As it turns out, I had a knack for fishing. Who knew? The best part about catching fish was that I was the only one using a cheap toy fishing pole and fake bait—fake because Liz and Charlie had so often forced my face into mud pies and tried to make me eat worms that even the sight of them made me physically ill. Needless to say, my sisters were annoyed that I caught more fish than they did.

After fishing, it started to grow dark, so we looked for a good place to set up camp. Lake Cumberland is a large lake, and somewhere on the lake was a tiny island where we docked for the night. We didn't want to go too far from the boat, so we set up camp about twenty yards from shore. As Mom and Dad worked, my sisters and I lay on our sleeping bags and gazed up at the stars. The summer night sky was beautifully lit. Instead of being only a state away from home, we felt as if we were oceans away. In our small town you couldn't see half the stars you could see at the lake. For this reason we named the island Paradise Island.

After roasting marshmallows and making s'mores, it was time for bed. Almost instantly after Liz, Charlie, and I had climbed into our tent, my sisters began to torment me.

"I sure hope the lake monster doesn't come and eat you tonight," Liz said to me as she walked past me and shook my legs as if she were the lake monster trying to drag me away.

"I heard Nessie was spotted here last summer," Charlie teased me as she lay down next to me.

"Shut up!" I screamed at the two of them as I buried my head under my pillow and tried not to listen to their scary stories. I kept my eyes shut and tried to lie very still hoping to trick my sisters into thinking I was asleep so they'd leave me alone. After some time had passed, they stopped tormenting me and reminisced about the fun they'd had that day. I lay quietly listening in wishing for once they'd include me in a normal conversation.

Before falling asleep, Liz and Charlie needed to go to the bathroom. Liz gently shook me to see if I needed to go with them. She knew I'd be too afraid to stay in the tent alone and would worry if I woke up and they weren't there. Despite always picking on me, they did occasionally look after me.

Liz was right; I didn't want to be left alone. We all put on our flip-flops, grabbed our flashlights, and left the tent. Although there was a small toilet in the cabin under the front end of the boat and we all had flashlights, my sisters decided it was too dark to get close to the water. They didn't want to risk anyone falling into the lake, so they decided to just use the woods.

We found a big tree close behind our tent. Charlie was the first to go to the bathroom behind the tree. After she finished, she stood next to me, and we both waited for Liz. As we waited, I pointed my flashlight up into the trees and looked around. I felt something gently brush against my foot.

I quickly shook my foot and immediately blamed Charlie. "Stop that, Charlie! It's not funny!" I said as I pointed my flashlight towards her face.

Charlie looked perplexed. "Stop what?" she asked in a defensive tone.

"Stop tickling my foot; I know it's you," I said in a firm voice. I had had enough of my sisters' torturing for one day.

"I'm not doing anything, Em!" she defended herself. "I swear!"

Suddenly something cold and wet touched the top of my foot. I stood frozen in fear. By the look on my face Charlie knew something was wrong. She quickly pointed her flashlight down at the ground and gasped. I was too afraid to look down.

"Em," she said in a scared, quiet tone, "whatever you do, don't move," she instructed.

I gulped as I stood as still as a statue and tried not to pee in my pants. Chills went up my spine as the cool, wet object moved slowly across my foot. After my foot was free from the eerie coolness, I built up enough courage to slowly move my flashlight and looked down at my feet. There on the ground near where both Charlie and I stood were snakes—big fat snakes, little skinny snakes. Snakes were all around the tree we had decided to pee behind. With my first glance at the snake nest I felt lightheaded and paralyzed with fear.

Charlie was the first to speak. "Liz," she said louder than a whisper but not too loud, "you might want to hurry up"

Luckily, Liz had finished her business and was walking our way. Before I could react, in one swift motion Charlie swooped me from the pile of snakes forming around my feet, sat me down on her opposite side, and yelled, "Snakes! Run!" as she pulled my hand and yanked me alongside her.

Liz began to scream as she discovered the snakes and ran faster than I've ever seen her run. We didn't stop running and screaming until we reached Mom and Dad's tent. Dad tore open the tent and yelled, "Girls! What's wrong?"

"Snakes!" Liz screamed.

"Tons of snakes!" Charlie added.

"Where?" Mom, who was now standing beside Dad, asked.

"Back there," Liz pointed behind us as she bent over and tried to catch her breath.

"What were you doing in the woods?" Dad asked.

I was finally over the shock of the snakes and decided to speak: "We had to pee!"

"They're just water snakes." Dad put his hand on my shoulder. "They won't hurt you. Let's all go back to our tents and try to get some sleep."

"The tent will be zipped, and the snakes won't be able to get inside," Mom said, "so you'll be safe while you sleep."

"I'm not sleeping in the tent!" Liz insisted.

"Me neither!" Charlie agreed, "not with all those snakes around!"

I just crossed my arms and shook my head no. If my sisters were too scared to sleep in the tent, I sure as heck wasn't going to sleep in there either.

So despite it being dark and late, Mom and Dad gathered all our stuff and carried it down to the boat. Our parents slept on the small bed in the cabin, Liz slept on one of the side benches, and Charlie and I shared the other side bench. For added protection Dad zipped the mesh boat cover. We were cozy and could hardly move, but at least we knew we were sleeping in a snake-free zone.

After that night, Charlie and Liz stopped picking on me for being afraid of swimming in snake-infested water, and the next day we spent most of our time on the torpedo or fishing instead of swimming.

After returning home from our first boating adventure, the whole family spent the week counting down days until we could get *Blue Beauty* back on the water. Dad even lightened up a little and let us girls play on the boat as long as he was outside with us. While Liz would lie on the bench and sunbathe, Charlie and I would stand on the back of the boat pretending to catch fish or competing to see who could cast the farthest. Meanwhile, Dad would do his daily boat prep and then kick back in his captain's chair and listen to Jimmy. Not only did the McCoy Boys become lake folk that summer but we also became "parrot heads" a.k.a. Jimmy Buffett fans. By the end of the summer, we knew how to boat, we knew how to camp, we knew how to fish, and we knew every Jimmy Buffett song word for word. Dad couldn't have been more proud of his McCoy Boys!

McCoy Christmas Traditions

December of my fourth-grade year had finally arrived. Growing up, the month of December was my favorite month. Not only did we get two weeks off from school to go sledding, build snow forts, and have snowball fights, but also it was the month of my favorite holiday—Christmas!

As a child, I had convinced myself that I was part elf. After all, I did fit the profile: unusually small compared to everyone else my age, extremely jolly (despite my two unruly sisters), and I possessed the uncanny ability to wrap a present perfectly. My gift wrapping skills, coupled with my being so good at keeping secrets, meant that in the weeks leading up to Christmas, Mom would let me stay up late and be her special gift wrapping assistant. My tiny fingers were just the right size to hold the ribbon in place while she'd tie and curl the ribbon on my sisters' presents. As a result of having helped her, I knew most of Charlie's and Liz's presents, but I never let on to knowing their gifts or mine and Mom's secret. Even as a young child, I didn't want to spoil the element of surprise that came with unwrapping Christmas presents. Seeing the excitement on my sisters' faces when they opened their gifts on Christmas morning, along with the excitement of receiving my own presents, was the best part of Christmas.

Growing up McCoy, December was full of family traditions that even as adults we still carry on. In my opinion, there's no better month to make homemade Chex Mix, Mom's beer cheese, and Christmas cookies. My sisters and I are never too old to gather at Mom's house to help her hang all her Christmas decorations and our hand-knitted stockings on the fireplace while listening to Charlie Brown Christmas music. For us, Christmas isn't Christmas without bundling up in warm winter clothes to walk the Cincinnati Zoo in the dark while we sip hot chocolate and ooh and ah over their light display while Christmas music is played over the loudspeakers. If the zoo's light display wouldn't put us in the holiday spirit, nothing would.

Last but not least is my most favorite McCoy tradition—cutting down a live Christmas tree at The Big Tree Plantation, a Christmas tree nursery about forty minutes north of our house. This was never a quick or easy trip, but in the end it was always worth the effort. For my family, "Christmas Tree Day" was guaranteed to be a fun-filled family adventure.

We'd start off our car ride to the plantation by listening to Christmas music while snacking on homemade Chex Mix and sipping hot cocoa from our thermoses. Upon arrival, we'd take a horse-drawn sleigh ride to the section of the nursery where trees were being sold. This was one of my favorite parts of the day, especially when there were several inches of snow on the ground and snow was still falling. Listening to the horse's feet clip-clop through a wonderland of snow would transport me to another place. No longer was I in Cincinnati, Ohio, on my way to pick out a tree; instead, I was at the North Pole on my way to help my fellow elves in Santa's workshop. When I finished my elf duties for the day, I'd head over to the stables to feed and play with my favorite reindeer, Rudolph. Every year while on that sleigh, I'd imagine a different elf adventure.

This plantation was magical! Not only did the nursery sell trees but they also had a stable full of live reindeer, a life-size manger scene, and a gift shop with a special section where kids could shop for inexpensive but fun things for family and friends.

After getting off the sleigh, my sisters and I would spend at least an hour walking around the nursery—often in the cold snow and sometimes ice—in search of the perfect McCoy Christmas tree. Unlike most families who wanted a perfect full and beautiful tree, my sisters and I liked to find the most unwanted tree on the lot so we could give it a good and loving home. One year our tree was so small and pitiful, it could only hold half of our ornaments. The other half remained untouched in our storage bin. That was the year of the Charlie Brown Christmas tree. Another year, our tree was so short and round that it hardly fit through the front door. We named that tree Big Bertha in honor of our favorite Myrtle Beach arcade game.

On this day, by the time we finally agreed upon a tree—one that was missing most of its branches on one side—our hands and feet were practically frozen, even through our gloves and thick wool socks! Picking out a tree, however, was only the beginning of our adventure; next came the hard work—cutting down the tree. This was the first Christmas since Mom and Dad separated, and that meant Dad was not there to cut down the tree for us. This year the McCoy Boys would be responsible for cutting down the tree ourselves.

It was extremely cold and snowy. While we stood shaking and trying to warm up, Mom spread an old blanket on the frozen ground, crawled underneath the tree, and began sawing away. Ten minutes later, she was dripping sweat, and the tree was still standing with only a small dent in its cold, hard trunk. Dad always made it look so easy.

We weren't sure what to do. Charlie, being the strongest of the three of us, offered to help Mom. She lay down on the blanket and sawed but made it only halfway through the tree's trunk. Mom and Charlie took turns sawing for the next thirty minutes. They were sweating and exhausted, and Liz and I were human icicles. While Mom and Charlie took a break to wipe sweat from their faces, I approached the now leaning tree, wrapped my arms around the bare part and grabbed onto the trunk, and with all my might I tried to pull the tree towards the ground. It hardly budged. I was too small, and my gloves were too thick for me to maintain a tight grip, and I fell from the tree and hit the frozen ground with a thud. As I stood up and rubbed my sore bottom, Charlie and Liz laughed at my failed attempt. Although I hadn't been successful, Charlie liked my idea. She shoved me out of the way, took off her gloves, and grabbed the tree trunk. She began to angrily pull the tree towards the ground. With a loud crack the trunk snapped. Charlie then crawled underneath the tree and finished sawing until at last it fell over. As it fell, we clapped and yelled, "Timmmberrr!"

We loaded our tree onto the plantation's tree sled and pulled it through the maze of trees still waiting to be chosen and cut down. After we dropped off our tree at the trimming station, they tagged it with "McCoy" and gave us our pay ticket. We hopped on the next sleigh back to the Christmas shop where Mom would pay for our tree. As soon as the sleigh stopped, Charlie, Liz, and I ran inside the toasty warm Christmas shop as quickly as our cold bodies would allow. This time, instead of eagerly running towards the toys, my sisters and I ran straight towards the wood-burning stove to "defrost," as I used to say. Once warm again, we bought a bag of kettle corn and hot cocoa to share while we sat by the warm fire and laughed about my sloth-like strength and Charlie's Tarzan-like strength and how Dad had no trouble cutting down a tree. Although there were smiles on our faces, we all missed Dad.

After we got warm, we browsed the kids' shop and secretly bought Mom a thing or two. While Mom paid for the tree, we girls went outside to the reindeer stables and tried to figure out which one was Dasher, Dancer, Comet, etc. To our disappointment, there was no red-nosed reindeer, nor were they playing any reindeer games.

After we paid for the tree, a man working at the plantation dragged it to our minivan and threw it on top of the roof. We eagerly jumped in, ready to go home and decorate our tree. Mom threw the van into drive and began to leave. We didn't make it too far out of the parking lot when we heard rustling coming from the roof of the van, followed by a loud crashing sound. My sisters and I sat up and looked out the rear window to see our beloved Christmas tree lying in the parking lot behind us. We all gasped and then cracked up.

In the distance, running to rescue our tree, was the man who had helped us put it on top of our car. While Charlie, Liz, and I laughed at Mom for driving off before tying down the tree, the gentleman slowed his stride and tapped on Mom's window. "Excuse me, ma'am," he said breathlessly as Mom rolled down the window, "but you do realize you have to tie the tree down before you leave, right?"

Embarrassed, Mom jokingly said, "Well, considering that it's on the ground, I realize I must have forgotten," and let out a chuckle. Liz, Charlie, and I were laughing our heads off in the back seat.

"If you'll hand me your ropes, I'll tie the tree down for you," the man said as he extended his hand through Mom's window.

Mom looked around on the passenger's side floorboard, and then turned to us in the back. "Girls, do you see any rope anywhere?" she asked.

We shook our heads no.

The man was kind enough to find some rope and show Mom how to anchor our tree to the roof of the van. In the years that followed, we never quite mastered the art of cutting down and transporting a live Christmas tree.

The Scrooge Sisters

The week of Christmas had finally arrived. In a few short days we'd be unwrapping our presents and celebrating the holiday with the entire family. All we had to do was behave for a couple more days while Apple watched us and Mom worked then Christmas would be here!

One morning while Mom was getting ready for work, the phone rang. It was Apple. She was sick with a cold and wouldn't be able to watch us girls that day. She didn't want any of us to catch whatever she had and risk being sick on Christmas. Mom understood but wasn't sure who she could get to watch us on such short notice. This was her first Christmas as a single mom, and she didn't want to take off from work because she had already put in for vacation after Christmas so she could have time with us before we went back to school. In order for her to take off then, she couldn't stay home with us now. She needed to go into the office.

Mom didn't want to be late for work, so she made a quick executive decision: she decided to leave Liz in charge for the day and treat this as a trial run for the upcoming summer vacation. We were shocked. Mom was going to leave us at home for the day, by ourselves, without an adult. We knew this was an important trial run, and we couldn't do anything to mess it up. Mom gave us all a quick kiss on the forehead, told us to be on our best behavior, and was out the door. She worked only a few minutes away and could be home in no time if we had an emergency.

As soon as the door shut, Liz and Charlie squealed with excitement and started dancing a little "we're-home-alone" jig.

I too was excited until I realized that this was the perfect opportunity for my sisters to do whatever they wanted to do to me without getting caught. Being unsupervised, my sisters would likely spend the entire day picking on me. I hung my head low in anticipation of what was to come. As it turned out, my sisters indeed had a plan that they had been waiting to put into action.

When Liz and Charlie finished their celebration, we headed downstairs to the kitchen to make ourselves breakfast. I was starving. I had been looking forward to Apple's bacon, scrambled eggs, and jelly toast that she always made us. When Apple cooked, she cooked with real butter and bacon grease, making her food taste much better than Mom's cooking.

"What would you like for breakfast, Em?" Liz asked a little too cheerfully. She was on a natural high from having been left in charge for the day.

"I want Apple's eggs," I pouted.

"Well," Charlie piped in, "you know what's better than Apple's eggs—something Mom never lets us eat?" she asked wide-eyed.

I shrugged my shoulders. All I wanted was for Apple to walk through the door, make me the breakfast I'd been looking forward to, then spend the day playing with me and keeping my sisters from picking on me.

"Cinnamon sugar toast!" Charlie beamed as she and Liz began to jump up and down in excitement again.

Cinnamon sugar toast? I hadn't had cinnamon sugar toast before, but it sounded good. I couldn't help but notice that, at least in this moment, my sisters were being nice to me instead of being mean. This was very unusual, seeing as how there were no parents or adults around forcing them to include me.

Liz and Charlie got to work. Liz put two pieces of white bread in the toaster then poured a glass of orange juice while Charlie combined cinnamon and sugar in a bowl and mixed it using a fork. Once the toast popped up, they each buttered a slice of bread and sprinkled the cinnamon sugar powder all over it. I watched the cinnamon and sugar dissolve into the melted butter, turning it dark brown. My mouth watered as a wonderful aroma filled the room. It smelled delicious. Then my sisters did something I never dreamed they would do: they walked the glass of orange juice and plate of cinnamon sugar toast over to the breakfast bar and placed them in front of me. They were serving me instead of making me serve them! This was a first. Normally my sisters did everything in their power—including cough, sneeze, or lick their food—to avoid having to share with me. Instantly I knew they wanted something from me, but the question was what.

As I sunk my teeth into my first bite of the buttery, cinnamon sugar deliciousness, my taste buds went crazy! It was so sweet. No wonder Mom never let us eat anything like this—which made me wonder how Charlie and Liz knew how to make this toast. Had one of them had a piece at a friend's house then come back home and made it for the other? Or was this a creation they invented on their own? Maybe they snuck out of bed in the middle of the night while Mom and I were sound asleep and quietly tip-toed into the kitchen to secretly enjoy the toast together. Liz and Charlie sat across the breakfast bar watching me enjoy every single bite without saying a word. I couldn't shake the feeling that, although they were being nice to me, they were up to no good.

"What do you guys want from me?" I asked in between bites. I was halfway finished with my second piece of toast. I wanted to make sure I ate all of my breakfast before they had a chance to change their minds and take my toast from me.

"Who?" Liz dramatically put her hand against her chest.

"Us?" Charlie asked.

"What makes you think we want anything from you?" Liz inquired.

"Because you're being nice to me," I said as I licked the cinnamon sugar goo off my fingers, "and you're only nice to me when you want something from me!"

"That's not true!" Charlie said as she looked at Liz and pretended to be offended.

"We're nice to you!" Liz said. "Well, some of the time," she added as she shrugged her shoulders, looked at Charlie, and they both laughed.

"Well, Em, you're smarter than we thought you were!" Charlie admitted.

"Wow, thanks, Charlie!" I said. I knew my sisters thought I wasn't as smart as they were, but hearing them say it was hurtful.

"Okay, here's the deal," Liz said, getting straight to the point, "We know you helped Mom wrap our Christmas presents."

"How do you know that?" I asked. I was surprised to know that my sisters knew Mom's and my little secret. I hadn't said anything to either of them, and I'm sure Mom hadn't either.

"Because you're the only third-grader who knows who Johnny Carson is," Charlie said.

I looked at her confused. I didn't know how my watching the late night show had anything to do with their knowing that I helped Mom wrap their Christmas presents.

Charlie continued: "Liz and I both know that the only time Mom has time to wrap our presents is after we're asleep. This Christmas break, Mom has let you stay up late with her while she shoos Liz and me off to bed. And Mom only lets you stay up if you help her with chores—like folding laundry and—," Charlie looked at me willing me to verify that what she was saying was true, "wrapping Christmas presents," she concluded.

Everything Charlie had just said was true. *Man, why did my sisters have to be so smart?*

"So," Liz said, "we want to know where she keeps the secret stash of Christmas presents!" Her eyes lit up with exhilaration.

The pit that had formed in my stomach as soon as Mom walked out the door was now consuming me. Whatever my sisters wanted with the Christmas presents couldn't be good, and as was the case with most of my sisters' plans, I wanted nothing to do with this plan.

I looked down and avoided eye contact with my sisters. I knew if I looked them in the eye, they would be able to tell I was lying.

"I don't know where she keeps the presents."

"Yes, you do," Charlie said as she got up from the kitchen barstool and stood next to me. "And you're going to show us," she insisted as she lifted my head up so she could see my eyes. Her big green eyes were shiny bright with no-good mischief. She meant business.

I began to panic. Charlie could clobber me at any moment. I was trying to hold back the tears as I wished Apple would somehow magically appear and save me. I knew this day was going to be awful.

"Please don't hurt me!" I begged Charlie as I willed myself not to cry.

"You think we're stupid enough to hurt you?" Charlie sounded offended. "If we left any marks on you, Mom would never let us stay home alone again."

"Charlie," Liz snapped, "don't be mean to Em. Em, we're not going to hurt you." Liz was now standing on the other side of me giving me a reassuring pat on the shoulder.

"But we do have a secret weapon to help persuade you to be our assistant for the day," Charlie said in a sly voice.

As Charlie ran upstairs, I looked to Liz with pleading eyes, begging her not to let Charlie do whatever it was she was planning to do to me. Usually while Charlie picked on me, Liz looked out for me. I could tell she didn't enjoy picking on me as much as Charlie did. However, today Liz was too deeply involved in Charlie's plan. They were on a mission to find their Christmas presents, and nothing was going to stop them.

When Charlie returned to the kitchen, an evil grin spread across her face. She was holding a large plastic bag. She opened a kitchen drawer, grabbed the salad tongs, then slowly approached Liz and me. Charlie used the tongs to grab an object from her bag of torture. Before I knew what had hit me, my stomach was churning from a repulsive smell. Dangling in front of my face was a pair of Dad's dirty and very smelly socks. A moment later, I was lying on the family room floor with Charlie sitting on top of me and Liz waving those wretched socks in my face. Charlie held my arms so I couldn't plug my nose shut. It didn't matter how hard I kicked or how loudly I screamed; no one was there to save me from my sisters.

After what seemed like an eternity of gagging from the smell, and as tears streamed down my cheeks and snotty boogers slid out from my nose, I couldn't take any more; I caved. "Okay," I sobbed, "I'll tell you!" I didn't want to give in, but I had no choice; I was only seconds away from throwing up.

Liz removed the socks from my face and allowed me to speak.

"Where's Mom's stash?" Charlie asked. She was still sitting on top of me with my arms pinned to my sides.

"In the crawl space," I sobbed. Now that my sisters knew where their presents were hidden, I doubted they'd actually go into the crawl space to get them. None of us girls ever dared to enter the crawl space; it was far too creepy.

Charlie eagerly jumped up off of me, Liz quickly shoved Dad's socks back into the Ziploc bag, and both raced to the laundry room where there was a tiny door to the crawl space. I had been wrong; apparently Liz and Charlie would enter the crawl space if it meant getting their Christmas presents.

I slowly sat up and wiped tears from my eyes and snot from under my nose. As I walked to the bathroom to blow my nose, I was surprised to see Liz and Charlie standing in front of the crawl space door. Given the speed at which they'd rushed to the laundry room, I had assumed that by now they'd be out of the crawl space with an arm full of presents.

"Em," Charlie grinned, "just the girl we were looking for…" she said as she approached me.

"What do you want now?" I sniffled.

"You're the smallest," Liz explained, "so you'll fit better in the crawl space."

"But—" I began.

"No buts!" Charlie snapped as she took another step towards me. "Get into that crawl space, or endure the wrath of the stinky socks!" Charlie said as she pointed to Liz, cuing her to hold up the bag of socks for me to see.

"Humph," I sighed as I hung my head low. Mom had been gone for no more than thirty minutes, and already I had almost puked and had the socks of death dangled in my face. And now it looked as if I would be forced into the scary crawl space. Could this day get any worse?

I wasn't moving quickly enough for my sisters, so they both gave me a little shove towards the crawl space door. I slowly got down on my hands and knees and looked into the dark, small crawl space. I could faintly see the light bulb hanging to the far left side, but it was turned off.

"Don't I get a light?" I turned to look at my sisters. I hadn't been in the crawl space before and didn't know where the pull to the light was.

Liz was the only one to respond. She walked over to the shelving unit in the laundry room and grabbed a flashlight, turned it on, and handed it to me.

I shined the light into the crawl space and immediately I could see the Christmas presents stacked in the far right corner. I took a big deep breath and began to crawl one-handed while holding the flashlight in the other hand. Since it was daytime and my sisters were sitting at the crawl space door waiting for their presents, I wasn't too scared. I just wanted to get the presents to my sisters so I could go upstairs to the living room and watch TV alone. I would leave my two evil sisters to their plan. But something inside me told me that my sisters weren't going to let me off that easily.

Once I reached the presents, I set the flashlight upright on the cool concrete floor so I could see what I was doing. I tried to focus on the presents and not the fact that there were spider webs all over the ceiling. I hated spiders. I wondered if there were other creatures—like mice—living in the crawl space. I shuddered then reassured myself that Mom wouldn't leave our Christmas presents anywhere where a rodent could destroy them. I worked quickly, crawling back and forth between the stack of presents and the crawl space entrance while I pushed Liz and Charlie's presents towards the door. Charlie and Liz took turns crawling into the entry way to retrieve each present. Several minutes later I was done, or so I thought.

As I began to crawl towards the door, Liz stopped me. "Not just our presents—yours too," she said with a smile on her face.

"But I don't want my presents now; I want them on Christmas," I protested. (Growing up in a middle-class family with three girls, the only time we received presents was on our birthday and at Christmas. Was I eager to unwrap my presents? Absolutely! However, Christmas was my favorite holiday, and I didn't want to ruin any of Mom's surprises. Even at a young age, I enjoyed the anticipation leading up to unwrapping our presents on Christmas morning. The older I got, as my sisters would tear through their presents, I'd admire the pretty wrapping paper and the ribbons on mine before unwrapping them.)

"Just do it, Emily!" I heard Charlie scream from behind Liz somewhere in the laundry room.

I grabbed a couple of my presents, pushed them towards the door for my sisters to retrieve, grabbed the flashlight, and came out of the crawl space and into the laundry room. As I stood up, I dusted off my pajama pants and looked around expecting to see all the presents and my sisters standing there, but to my surprise, I was the only one in the empty laundry room. I shut the crawl space door and walked into the family room where I saw my sisters sitting on the floor next to three stacks of presents and Mom's plastic bin of gift wrapping supplies. They had been busy while I was in the crawl space.

"Join us!" Charlie said joyfully.

Reluctantly, I sat down next to Liz. Not only had my sisters managed to bring out all the presents from the laundry room and sort them by name into three stacks, but also they had found Mom's gift wrap bin in her room. They had made three plates of cinnamon sugar toast and had a mini pile of candy sitting in between the plates of toast. My eyes grew wide as I examined the pile of candy—lemon heads, flying saucers, peanut M&M's, candy dots, and Mary Jane chews—all of my favorite candy! From the look of things, my sisters had been planning this moment for some time now and had been waiting for just the right opportunity to set their plans into motion.

My sisters had a way of always keeping me on my toes. Within minutes they had gone from torturing me with smelly socks to making me more cinnamon sugar toast. They were always confusing me—mean one minute, nice the next. I always wondered if this behavior was normal for siblings, or if there was something wrong with Charlie and Liz. I knew they weren't going to share any of their candy with me, but I was grateful to see three plates of cinnamon sugar toast. And thankfully, no socks of torture were to be seen!

"So, here's what we're going to do," Charlie said. "We know you helped Mom wrap all our presents, and Liz and I don't want to wait until Christmas to find out what Mom bought us this year, so we're going to very carefully slice open the tape on one side of each present just enough so that we can peek inside to read the writing on the side of the boxes, but if we mess up the wrapping paper, we need you to help us re-wrap it exactly—and I mean exactly—like Mom had it so she doesn't find out."

I just sat in my place staring at Charlie. Her plan sounded insane to me, but I had learned my lesson for the day and knew better than to argue or disagree with her.

Liz added, "All of Mom's presents have ribbon wrapped around the gift with a bow attached, so if we need to take off the bow, we'll need you to help us make a new one exactly like Mom's. And if you're good and help us, we'll reward you with candy!"

Charlie added, "If you're bad and don't help us, we'll hold you down and get the socks back out. Understand?" she asked.

I swallowed hard and nodded my head that I understood. I knew that one way or another my sisters would get their way. When given a choice between helping them and being rewarded with my favorite candy, or not helping them and having Dad's smelly socks rubbed into my face, the choice was a no-brainer. I didn't want to help them with their no-good plan, and I felt completely guilty that I played a part in their opening their presents without Mom here to see. Mom was always telling us girls that it brought her so much joy to watch us unwrap our presents on Christmas morning. She reminded us that Christmas is about giving and seeing other people's joy. I might be the youngest, but I knew this was an awful idea.

Charlie was the first to test their unwrapping plan. She checked to make sure there was more green ribbon in Mom's bin, tore off the ribbon, then examined her package to find the perfect side to unwrap. She picked the side of the package where the bottom and top creases of the wrapping paper were held together by a single piece of tape. That way when she re-taped the package, the original piece of tape would be hidden. If she was precise in smoothing the second piece of tape, it wouldn't look suspicious. Very carefully she opened the scissors and used one side to slowly and precisely cut a straight line through the middle of the tape holding the folded pieces of wrapping paper together. I watched in disbelief as Charlie slowly and carefully lifted up each flap of the wrapping paper until the side of the gift was exposed. I held my breath. It was intense watching her deliberately break Mom's rule. I wondered if Santa would put her on the naughty list and skip her this year.

"Yes!" she screamed excitedly, "a Polaroid camera—just what I asked for!" she beamed.

I let out a loud sigh as I began to breathe normally again. Thankfully, she hadn't destroyed the wrapping paper. Now all she had to do was re-wrap the gift. I worked quickly to make Charlie a new green bow and handed it to her. In exchange she gave me a Mary Jane.

After she knew what her gift was, she slowly and carefully re-folded the paper and used a piece of tape identical in size to the original piece of tape that she had slit open. She placed the new piece of tape on top of the original piece and then smoothed it with her fingertip. She then wrapped a piece of green ribbon around the package, and I held my finger on the ribbon as she tied the bow. She examined her work. "Good as new!" she smiled. She set the present aside so she would know she had already opened that one.

Liz was the next to go, and just like Charlie, she would need to cut off a bow. She checked Mom's gift wrap bin to make sure she had the same gold ribbon. Luckily, there was one spool of gold ribbon left in Mom's bin. Liz cut the ribbon off the package then proceeded to execute the process Charlie had modeled for her.

"I knew it!" she cheered with joy. "I've been asking for a makeup caboodle!" Liz smiled ear to ear.

When it was time to place the bow back on, I quickly made a gold ribbon identical to Mom's, and Liz rewarded me with Peanut M&M's. I sat there and watched my sisters unwrap presents while I ate candy. I felt guilty that Mom was working while we were being bad and having a fake Christmas morning without her; however, seeing my sisters so happy and being rewarded with candy wasn't so bad. Even though my sisters were blackmailing me and making me work for candy, at least they were including me in their fun. We spent the rest of the morning unwrapping and rewrapping presents. There was magic in the air that morning. We were having fun without bickering or fighting. It felt as if it really were Christmas morning, except we were missing two very important people—Mom and Dad.

After we finished having our fake Christmas morning, we made sure to clean up our mess so Mom wouldn't find a single clue revealing our misbehavior. Liz grabbed a black garbage bag from the laundry room, and we picked up all the bows we had to cut off the packages and placed them in the black garbage bag. Instead of leaving the bag in our kitchen trash can, Charlie took it to the outside trash can.

Next, I crept back into the crawl space, and my sisters handed me the presents. I re-stacked them neatly in the corner in the same way I had found them. Lastly, we put all the scissors and spools of ribbon back into Mom's gift wrap bin and put it back into her bedroom closet.

We had managed to do all of this before lunchtime. We had a feeling Mom would come home for lunch to check in on us, and indeed she did. A few minutes before noon, we sat on the living room couch, turned on the TV, and nervously waited for Mom to come home. I imagined her walking through the door and immediately having her sixth sense kick in. She'd figure out what we had been up to all morning and cancel Christmas. To our surprise, Mom didn't notice a thing. After greeting her with a hug, we all headed down to the kitchen for lunch. Liz, Charlie, and I were full from all the cinnamon sugar toast and candy we had just eaten, but we forced down some turkey sandwiches so Mom wouldn't suspect a thing.

That night, we went to bed with stomach aches from all the sugar we had eaten. Serves us right! When Mom tucked us in, she told us how proud she was of us for being good to one another on our first day with Liz in charge. As I lay in bed willing myself to sleep, I couldn't stop the tears from trickling down my face. Had Mom known the truth, she would have been so disappointed in us. I felt awful.

A few days later, it was Christmas Eve. Us McCoy Boys were more than wound up and ready for the party of the year! Every Christmas Eve, Mom's sister—our Aunt Anne—and her husband Scott hosted the biggest and best party. Mom's entire side of the family would gather at their house for dinner, drinks, and a gift exchange and then at end of the evening, while Apple watched all the grandkids play with their new toys, the adults would play cards in the basement.

Anne and Scott's house sat back in the woods down a long, winding gravel driveway and was a Christmas wonderland. This year the driveway was covered in two inches of snow, and their house was brightly lit with an elaborate light display. (We referred to Mom's side of the family as "the wealthy ones." They could splurge on Christmas lights and decorations all throughout the house.) Upon entering, we saw the dining room table lined with all kinds of delicious food that us McCoy Boys only had the pleasure of enjoying on Christmas Eve. The party spread included, but was not limited to, shrimp and cocktail sauce; homemade beer cheese dip, a hometown favorite; Grippo's Bar-B-Q Potato Chips; coleslaw; turkey sandwiches; a fruit and veggie tray; tiny sweet pickles; all different kinds of olives; a big pot of barbecue... The list went on and on, and that was only what was on the dining room table! There was another table in the kitchen full of desserts—Santa sugar cookies with red frosting and sprinkles, chocolate chip cookies, chocolate walnut brownies, rice crispy treats cut into the shape of Christmas trees—and on the stove, hot chocolate ready to serve. Between all of Anne and Scott's Christmas decorations, the food and desserts, and the kids' gift exchange, Christmas Eve was truly a magical evening.

When everyone was finished eating, we'd gather in the living room for the gift exchange. While we waited our turn to unwrap a present, we'd eat candy canes off the huge, expensive-looking and elaborately decorated Christmas tree that always stood tall in the corner of the room. Each year we'd rotate who got to unwrap the first present. One year we'd start with the oldest grandchild, Margo, and work our way down to the youngest, Toby. On these years, I fell second to last in the line-up of nine. I watched enviously as Margo, then Liz, then Charlie, then Penny, then Lynn, then Jon, then finally Lauren unwrapped their presents. It felt as if an eternity passed before my turn finally arrived. However, the following year, we'd start with the youngest and end with the oldest. Those were my favorite years! I was second to unwrap my present and could hardly contain my excitement as I watched Toby unwrap the first gift. Oh, to be a child on Christmas Eve again!

After opening presents, all the grandchildren would stay in the living room playing with each other's new toys while the parents gathered in the basement for an exciting evening of gambling. Within minutes, the table where the kids had eaten dinner was transformed into a mini Vegas casino. With a twenty-five-cent ante, a two-dollar burn, and twenty adults playing, the pot could get rather large. This year, however, Charlie was tired of watching the adults win all the money and wanted in on some extra Christmas cash. Having received mostly clothes during the gift exchange, she grew bored and came up with a clever idea to have a little fun while earning some cash.

Charlie recruited Liz, Margo, and Penny to test her money making idea. They stayed upstairs and allowed some time to pass while the parents played cards in the basement. After about thirty minutes, the four of them headed downstairs, each holding a red Solo cup with the word "Tips" written on the side.

They circled the card table asking the adults if they could get them a fresh drink, a small plate of food, or a dessert. Being so involved in the card game and not wanting to get up for another beer or glass of wine, they all said yes and gave them their orders. The four of them ran back upstairs to the kitchen, prepared all the orders, and then went back downstairs and delivered the food and drinks. Upon delivery they held up their tip cups, and all the adults chuckled. Everyone playing had piles of quarters and a stack of one-dollar bills. They all threw a couple of quarters into each of their tip cups and continued with their game. Charlie's idea was a success!

Every thirty minutes or so, the four of them would head back downstairs and take more orders. However, instead of running upstairs to fill orders, they made Jon, Lauren, and me stand at the top of the basement steps and yelled orders up to us. We would then go to the kitchen, fill the orders, and bring them downstairs. At the end of the night, they gave us each one dollar. I'm sure they kept most of the tip money for themselves.

The night would end with all the kids excited about their new toys from the gift exchange and from Apple. We'd load up our new toys along with a baggie full of cookies to take home. Although the night was over for most of Mom's family, it wasn't over for us McCoy Boys; we had one more stop to make—our church. (Midnight mass has always been my favorite mass of the year. The entire church is lit with candles, and the aisles are lined with poinsettias. For me there is something calming about walking in from the dimly lit, snowy parking lot and entering the candle-lit church. I love how the candlelight reflects off the stained glass church windows. It is so beautiful.)

After all the excitement from the party, Liz, Charlie, and I were wide-eyed for about the first half of the mass. We secretly brought in cookies and pieces of candy canes that we had taken from the party and stored in our coat pockets. I'm sure Mom saw us, but she didn't say anything. She let us eat our treats and pretended not to notice. After our candy stash ran out, and the closer to one o'clock it became, we began to nod off in the church pew. Mom gave us a gentle nudge to wake us up. We stayed until we received communion then quietly slipped out the side door. It was only a short, five-minute car ride home from church, but we were fading fast. Once Mom pulled into the driveway, Liz, Charlie, and I sleepily walked from the car into our house holding our new gifts. We left a cookie out for Santa then headed up to bed. (As a child, I loved the nervous excitement of going to sleep on Christmas Eve. Mom would read us *'Twas the Night Before Christmas* then tuck us into our beds. Many Christmas Eves, as we were falling asleep, I swear I heard the sound of eight tiny reindeer on our roof and the faint jingle of sleigh bells.)

When we woke up on Christmas morning, we all stood anxiously by our bedroom doors and waited until Mom gave us the go-ahead to run down the steps to the living room where our tree and presents awaited us. In the McCoy house, Santa didn't wrap the presents he left us; instead, his presents sat unwrapped in front of Mom and Dad's wrapped presents. We could tell whose were whose from Santa because Mom had sectioned the tree off into three distinct sections—one for each of us. Santa would leave his gifts in our designated sections. We could hardly contain our excitement as we examined our gifts from Santa then eagerly showed one another what the big guy had brought us. Santa never disappointed! He always brought the biggest and best gifts from our Christmas list that we knew Mom and Dad couldn't afford.

On this particular Christmas morning, after checking out the gifts from Santa, Mom turned on Charlie Brown Christmas music and grabbed a garbage bag to collect all the gift wrap then we began to unwrap presents from Mom—presents that Liz, Charlie, and I had unwrapped several days ago. Each of us took turns pretending to be surprised, but it was hard.

After we finished unwrapping our presents, we couldn't help but notice tears in Mom's eyes. "I'm sorry this isn't a big Christmas like it has been for you girls in the past. None of you seemed too excited with your gifts," Mom said as she wiped tears from her eyes.

We all looked at one another. Seeing how upset Mom was and hearing that she thought we didn't like our presents made me feel extremely guilty. Had she seen us a couple of days ago, she would have known how much we truly loved our gifts.

"I love all my presents, Mom," Liz said trying to reassure her. I could tell Liz was feeling guilty as well.

"Me too," Charlie agreed. And although she was agreeing with Liz, I could tell she wasn't as concerned as Liz and I were.

"Me three," I piped in feeling extremely guilty that (a) I'd helped my sisters with their plan, and (b) I'd ruined Christmas for Mom.

"It's just," Mom explained, "as a parent I look forward to seeing the joy on all your faces when you open your presents, and this year, something feels a little off. I know you got a lot of clothes, but with this being the first year your dad and I aren't together, money's a little tight."

Hearing how concerned Mom was made me want to smack my sisters for forcing me to be part of their plan. I looked up at Liz, who was now crying. I knew she had realized that not only had we taken away from our excitement on Christmas morning but also we had taken away from Mom's excitement as well.

I couldn't stand it any longer; I ran up to Mom and gave her a big hug and began to cry. "I'm sorry, Mom," I sobbed. "I didn't mean to ruin Christmas." I needed to confess.

"What?" Mom asked as she hugged me tightly. "You didn't ruin Christmas," she reassured me. "Why would you think that?"

I was ready to tell her the whole truth until Charlie came up behind me and joined in on the hug. "She doesn't know what she's saying," Charlie said as she bent over to give me a kiss on the back of my head and simultaneously whispered a threatening word—"socks"—into my ear. After kissing me, she said to Mom, "I think the reason Em, Liz, and I seem a little off is because this is a different Christmas than we're used to having—you know, without having Dad here this morning. And when Dad picks us up, we're going to miss you." Charlie said.

I began to cry harder. I wanted to tell Mom everything, but I knew if I did, my sisters—or at least Charlie—would never let me live it down. She would torture me with Dad's disgusting socks. There are a lot of things I have learned to endure, but germy, smelly socks is not one of them.

"Nothing's your fault, Em." Mom squeezed me tighter. "Now, now, it's okay. Everything will be fine. Let's all forget that I ever said anything and go eat our Christmas morning cinnamon rolls before your Dad picks you up," Mom said in a loving and reassuring voice.

As Mom released me from her arms, Liz quickly joined my side. Mom headed downstairs while we girls stayed back in the living room.

"What's wrong with you two?!" Charlie quietly snapped at Liz and me after Mom was out of hearing range.

"What's wrong with *us*?!" Liz snapped back. "What's wrong with *you*?! Didn't you see how upset Mom was?" Liz asked Charlie. "And it's all your fault for taking away the surprise of Christmas!" Liz said.

"Don't pretend like it was all my doing!" Charlie quietly yelled to Liz. "You and Emily are just as guilty as I am." Charlie was right; we were all guilty, but as we ate breakfast with Mom, we acted like we had done nothing wrong.

After breakfast, Dad picked us up, and we went to his apartment, where small piles of presents awaited us. As we unwrapped Dad's presents, anticipation filled us all. We were thoroughly surprised by all of Dad's presents. He had done well for his first year of Christmas shopping by himself.

Although we didn't get much from Dad, I realized that it was the thought he'd put into shopping for us that had made his gifts so special—that and the element of surprise. After unwrapping all our presents, the magnitude of what Charlie and Liz had done set in. Liz and I held our heads low as we looked over all our presents. I couldn't help but notice tears in Charlie's eyes as she excused herself and headed to the bathroom. That Christmas we all learned a valuable lesson. By being impatient and peeking at our presents before Christmas we had taken away the most important thing about Christmas morning: we had stolen some of the magic of Christmas and some of Mom's joy. My sisters had worked together to force me to help them carry out their awful plan—one that ultimately ruined Christmas morning, I couldn't help but hold a grudge against them. For the remainder of Christmas break, I referred to them as The Scrooge Sisters.

To this day, us McCoy Boys still celebrate Christmas Eve with Mom's side of the family—except the family is much bigger now. Now my sisters, cousins, and I are all grown with children of our own. We have graduated from waiting on our parents while they play cards to joining them at the card table while our children wait on all of us with their red Solo tip cups. Midnight mass is still my favorite mass, and Christmas is still my favorite holiday. Us McCoy Boys still cut down live Christmas trees at the Big Tree Plantation with Mom, and we get all bundled up with our kids and gather on cold winter nights to walk through the zoo and admire all the lights. And Christmas isn't Christmas without Mom's homemade beer cheese and Chex Mix. These family traditions hold a special place in my heart, and I am eternally grateful for my parents, grandparents, aunts, uncles, and cousins for making Christmas such a magical and memorable holiday for our family. I hope my daughters enjoy these traditions as much as I did—and still do—and that they will one day carry on the traditions with families of their own.

The Day the Game Went too Far

My sisters loved to play games with me. In the 1980s, most sisters enjoyed playing Barbies together. My sisters' version of playing Barbies was tying my Barbie to our toy train tracks while their Barbies sat aside cheering on the train. Or playing beauty parlor and cutting my Barbie's long blond hair until she was bald. Sometimes they wouldn't stop there. On occasion they would set fire to my poor Barbie's bald head just for fun. I never allowed myself to get too attached to my dolls.

Another one of their famous games was Concoction. While I sat blindfolded on the kitchen chair, Liz and Charlie would use five ingredients to make a "delicious" treat for me to eat—for example, a brown sugar Pop-Tart topped with pickle relish, mustard, a splash of hot sauce, and a slice of turkey. After they finished making their tasty creations, they would spoon-feed me small portions and give me several minutes to guess what five ingredients they had used to make the concoction. My prize for guessing the correct ingredients was that I wouldn't have to eat it! If I guessed incorrectly, I would be forced to eat all of it. We played this game until (a) they grew bored or (b) I grew nauseous.

By far the most memorable game we played was Great Escapes. The first summer Mom left Liz in charge instead of a babysitter, was the infamous summer that Great Escapes went too far.

While other kids on our block spent summer vacation riding bikes and playing tag outside, us McCoy Boys had been instructed by overly protective Mom not to go anywhere, not even in our own backyard, unless it was together. Instead of being upset at

Mom for this rule, my sisters looked at me as a nuisance who was ruining their summer vacation. Because my sisters were limited in what they could do during summer vacation, I became the source of their entertainment.

In this game Liz and Charlie would come up with various scenarios such as a burglar breaking into a house or an evildoer robbing a bank. In each scenario I would be the bad guy, and naturally, they were always the good guys. After I was captured, my sisters would tie me to a chair using various objects they found lying around the house—belts, scarves, hair ties, and ribbon. They'd even use duct tape, but that was only when they were feeling very loving.

Once I was securely tied to a chair, they'd time me to see how long it would take for me to escape. Surprisingly, I was good at escaping. I don't know if it was because my wrists were so small, or because it was hard for them to tightly secure the ties, or if the fear of being tied to a chair caused adrenaline to consume my body helping me to escape, but whatever was the case, I distinctly recall only having to say uncle a few times. As summer vacation passed, the more I suffered through playing Great Escapes, the faster I got at escaping. Liz and Charlie grew annoyed that their little sister was beating them at their own game.

One particular summer day, when Charlie was feeling extra-feisty, she decided it was time they stepped up their game. After I was tied to the chair of torture, as I liked to call it, Charlie instructed Liz to help her move the chair. Although Charlie was several years younger than Liz, Charlie was the mastermind behind all their games—not to mention, she was bigger and stronger than skinny, non-athletic Liz. Throughout the summer, although Mom had left Liz in charge, Liz was often forced to follow Charlie's orders. If she didn't, she knew Charlie could take her down whenever she wanted to.

I remember thinking *Now what?* as they moved the chair of torture closer to my side of the room.

"Get her closer to the bed," Charlie instructed as Liz struggled to hold up her side of the chair.

"Okay, now we're going to flip her over on top of her bed," Charlie ordered Liz.

"What?" I screeched as they flung me through the air and onto my bed. My screams were quickly muffled as I landed face down on top of the bed.

"Ow!" I whimpered. I was far from comfortable. "Come on, guys; this isn't funny!" I whined in a muffled voice as my face sank deeper into my mattress. My body fought the chair and tried to fall forward into the bed, but the ties pulled my body back in the opposite direction.

"Oh, we're not done!" I sensed mischief in Charlie's voice.

"Now what?" Liz asked Charlie in an annoyed voice.

Charlie walked across the room to her bed and grabbed her comforter. She brought it over to my bed and threw it on top of the chair. Suddenly everything went dark around me.

"Don't let her do this to me, Liz!" I pleaded through the muffled darkness.

I could hear the shuffling of feet as the comforter shifted on top of me. However, the blanket stopped when I heard a thud, followed by an "Ouch! Geez, Charlie!" I didn't have to see what had just happened to know that Liz had tried to rescue me only to have Charlie stop her with a swift punch in the arm. Liz would often try to save me, but Charlie could throw one wicked punch.

"This isn't right!" Liz scorned Charlie.

"Oh, she's fine." Charlie didn't sound the least bit concerned.

"Well, I don't want any part of this!" Liz screamed as I heard her storm out of the room.

"Don't leave me, Liz!" I pleaded as my face began to sweat under the hot comforter.

"Relax!" Charlie said nonchalantly. "Come on now, Em," she added in an encouraging voice, "I know you can escape!"

It was dark underneath the comforter, and half of my face had sunk into the mattress making it difficult to breathe. My palms were sweating, and my breathing began to quicken. I couldn't help but panic as I tried to break free from the chair, but the ties were too strong. The more I tried, the more my body fought back.

"I... I don't think I can." Anxiety filled my voice.

"Yes, you can; you're a Great Escapes pro! That's why we had to make it more challenging," Charlie said in an encouraging voice.

I could tell Charlie wasn't ready to give up on her mastermind game and therefore wasn't ready to release me. Her determination scared me more than anything, and I frantically tried to break free.

The more I tried to escape, the hotter it got beneath the comforter, and the more I began to sweat. My face was now dripping wet, and my eyes filled with tears. I felt as if I was going to suffocate with Charlie's comforter on one side of my face and mine on the other.

"Come on, Charlie," I began to cry, "it's getting hot under here!"

"Suck it up, Em! You can do this." Charlie sounded a bit annoyed with her whiny little sister.

After what seemed like several more minutes of trying to escape, but most likely was only seconds, I began to panic like I had never panicked before. Charlie wasn't giving up any time soon, and I didn't know how much longer I could last tied to a chair underneath a hot blanket. I was now sweating profusely and breathing fast and hard. Suddenly I began to see bright white spots.

"Lizzzzz!" I screamed, "Help me!"

As I began to breathe through my mouth and cry harder, I could hear my sisters fighting in my room. Suddenly their voices sounded as if they were being played in slow motion through a vocoder, and I was having trouble breathing. My body began to go limp as my ears began to ring and I started to see bright white spots. This would be the first time I would experience what it feels like to pass out.

By the time I came to, I was sitting on the floor with my back up against my bed and my head resting on the mattress. A blurry vision of Liz and Charlie slowly came into focus. They were both staring down at me with terrified expressions. Liz was holding a cup of ice water and Charlie, a wet wash cloth.

"[BLEEP], Em!" Liz exclaimed. Teenage Liz had what my dad liked to call a diarrhea mouth. Bad words seemed to flow uncontrollably from her mouth. "You scared the [BLEEP] out of me!" she said as Charlie leaned down and dabbed my forehead with the cool, wet washcloth.

"Eh, she's fine!" Charlie said nonchalantly.

I sat up and reached for the glass of water in Liz's hand. With shaking hands, I quickly drank the cool, refreshing water. Water had never tasted so good!

"Mom is going to kill us when she gets home!" Liz panicked as she paced the floor.

When I finished the cup of water, I placed the empty glass down beside me. As I took the wet washcloth and dabbed my sweaty wrists, I couldn't help but notice the faint red marks that encircled them.

As I stared at the red marks on my wrist, I could feel an uncontrollable anger growing inside me. I looked at both of my sisters. Liz had panic written all over her face. Charlie stared at me with a cool expression. When I spoke, I spoke slowly so my sisters would hear everything I had to say: "Never again will you tie me to a chair and put me upside down on my bed..." my voice grew angrier and louder, "...underneath a [BLEEPING] blanket!" I found myself screaming profanities that I had only heard adults and Liz say but never imagined coming out of my own mouth, as I furiously threw the wet washcloth at Charlie's smug face.

Stunned, my sisters stood frozen in their places, with their jaws hanging to the floor. Their kid sister, who had never cursed before, nor been this angry, had just screamed a profanity at them. They knew I meant business.

That night at dinner we all sat quietly as we picked at our food. When Mom asked how our day was, we all glanced at one another. My sisters said nothing as they waited for me to rat them out. (I never told my parents what my sisters did to me when they weren't around; they had trained me not to be a tattletale. The times I had told on them, my sisters sought revenge tenfold. In the middle of the night, they'd cut a small piece of my hair or ruin my favorite toy, or worse, cut a part of my baby blanket off. Telling on them was digging my own grave.)

I sighed as I looked down at my dinner plate and replied, "Nothing much—played outside, laid around and watched TV." I couldn't look Mom in the eye as I lied, so I looked up across the table at my sisters.

Charlie and Liz looked at each other in disbelief.

"Well, tomorrow I want you girls to go to the pool," Mom said. "I didn't pay for a pass for you girls to sit around and watch TV all summer!"

"Okay, Mom!" Liz replied a little too eagerly.

"We'll go tomorrow, Mom!" Charlie smiled and nodded in agreement.

Lying in bed that night, I couldn't sleep with the blanket anywhere near my face, or I would panic.

Charlie could hear my loud breathing from the other side of the room. "That was real cool of you not to rat us out," Charlie said.

"Never again, Charlie." I replied.

"I went too far this time. I'm sorry, Em." Sincerity filled her voice.

"I know," I sighed as I rolled onto my side, and tears trickled down my face.

"I do love you, sis." she said.

"Then don't try to kill me!" I let out a little chuckle as I wiped the tears from my face.

Even now, as an adult, I cannot sleep with the covers up past my chest without thinking about the day Great Escapes went too far.

Snap, Crackle, Pass Out

It was my sixth-grade year, and I was loving life. My friends and I lived for lunch and recess, which was by far the best forty-five minutes of the school day. Lunch was the perfect time to catch up on all the sixth-grade gossip, i.e. who had a crush on whom, and recess was a time to chase all the cute boys around the school yard, play kickball, wall ball, or tetherball. Ah, nothing better than growing up in the nineties, a time when kids actually played in the schoolyard instead of sitting in the schoolyard on their smartphones sending each other virtual board game moves via text message.

My best friend Nina and I were chasing boys around the playground during recess as we always did. Nina, who had been my best friend since kindergarten, was more than a head taller than me, and although she was skinny, she was much stronger than I was. After a while of chasing the boys, I grew tired and turned the corner of the playground to stop and take a breather. Here the boys wouldn't be able to see me resting up against the side of the building. What I didn't realize was that Nina was right behind me. As she turned the corner, she glanced back to make sure no boys were following us and, unaware that I had stopped running, she ran into me at full speed.

I didn't know what hit me. Before I knew it, I was flying forward. As I hit the hard concrete, I heard a loud snap, followed by instant pain shooting up my left arm. Tears filled my eyes as I tried to lift myself off the ground only to have my arm buckle. I looked down to see a mangled mess. I had somehow managed to break both my radius and my ulna completely in half. Not only were the bones broken but they had twisted in such a way that my arm looked like the letter "u"! The sight freaked me out! I began to panic and cry harder. My arm looked so messed up that I didn't think it could be fixed. I was pretty sure it was going to have to be amputated.

Luckily, Nina jumped into action. She reassured me that everything was going to be fine as she put her forearms in my armpits and pulled me up off the ground in one swift motion. Once I was upright, she yelled for the teacher's help and told me to keep my head down and close my eyes so I wouldn't see my arm.

Moments later, I was being carried to the nurse's office—yes, carried—because at this point I couldn't stop throwing up all over myself and the teacher. By the time we reached the nurse's office, I felt as if I was going to pass out. As I lay on the tiny cot in the nurse's office, I closed my eyes so I wouldn't have to see her wrap my disgusting arm in a sling. Before I knew it, Mom had arrived at school and rushed me to our children's hospital.

Although this wasn't my first trip to Children's ER, this was my first experience in the orthopedic department. I had to hold very still while they took several x-rays of my arm. After examining the x-rays, the doctor explained to Mom that the images confirmed his gut feeling: I needed immediate surgery to fix my arm.

Mom was a mess. None of her McCoy Boys had ever had surgery before. Leave it to me to be the first. Mom explained to the doctor that as a child, one of her neighbors had had his tonsils removed only to have a terrible reaction to the anesthetics leaving him mentally and physically challenged. She cried as she begged him to find a way to fix my arm without putting me under. That is not the story you want to share with your twelve-year-old daughter who is about to go under the knife for the first time. As if I wasn't scared enough to be having my first surgery, she had to add the fear of having some God-awful reaction to the anesthetics! (And people wonder where I get my anxiety.)

As Mom and the doctor went back and forth debating the best way to fix my arm, Mom pleaded with him, "Please, doctor, isn't there anything else you can try?"

"Well," he said, "we can try to manipulate her bones back into place, but there's no guarantee it will work."

The words "manipulate bones" got my attention. Not only did that phrase make the procedure sound excruciatingly painful; it sounded far worse than surgery! I looked at my arm and then back at the doctor and said, "I think I'll take the surgery, doc!" Too bad I was only twelve years old and didn't have any say in the matter.

Before I could get the doctor or Mom to consider my opinion, the room was full of medical staff. I didn't know why the doctor needed all the other people in the room, but my gut was telling me I wasn't going to like what was about to happen. The doctor had me lie down on the examining table, and before I knew it, the medical staff was all over me—one holding my head to the right so I wouldn't be able to witness the awful manipulation of my left arm and all the others holding my legs, right arm, and entire body down.

My eyes searched for Mom as I pleaded for surgery one last time. I didn't know what was about to happen, but I knew it wasn't going to be good.

"On the count of three," I heard the doctor say, "one… two… three," and then I felt my left arm being twisted in ways I never knew was possible. I heard a strange grinding and crackling noise as my bones were being forced back into their correct positions. A cool sweat formed on my face as my limp left arm was tugged and pulled in ways that yet again made me vomit. Before I knew it, I was seeing bright white dots, and I passed out from the pain.

When I came to, Mom was sitting in a chair at the side of my bed. She was holding my right hand and dabbing a cool washcloth on my forehead. I looked at my left arm to see a large white cast extending from my armpit all the way down to my hand. I wiggled my fingers and was surprised to see them respond.

"I thought you'd want purple," Mom said as tears trickled down her face, "but they said we could wait until you woke up to pick a color." Mom leaned over and gave me a gentle kiss on my forehead.

I still felt disoriented. Not only was my arm throbbing but so was my head. I was furious at Mom for allowing them to manipulate my bones back into place. At least with surgery I would have been put to sleep and wouldn't have had to experience such awfulness. I didn't want to speak to Mom or any of the doctors. I only nodded my head yes, confirming I wanted a purple cast. Mom notified one of the nurses that I was awake.

Mom and I sat in silence as they wrapped a purple layer around my white cast. In the weeks to follow, I came to secretly like my cast. Because I was limited to the use of one arm, Mom exempted me from household chores—not to mention, Charlie, Liz, and all my friends thought my purple cast was cool. They all signed it with a black Sharpie and helped carry my books and lunch around school.

When it was time to remove my purple cast, I'll never forget how weak, stinky, and hairy my left arm was. My arm hadn't healed all the way, so it was put in another cast. My second cast wasn't as big as my first one. It only extended from below my elbow to my hand and yes, it was also purple. After my second cast was removed, I had to have x-rays to confirm that both bones had properly healed. To my dismay, although the bones were healed, my arm was left permanently crooked.

In the years that followed, the instructors at cheer camp would yell at me to straighten my arm, and I'd have to explain that that was as straight as my arm would get. In gym class I could never bump a volleyball because it hurt too badly when the ball would hit the place where my bones had fused. In marching band I had to hold my drumsticks a different way than all the other drummers because of my crooked left arm. I know Mom thought she was doing what was best for me at the time, but I wish she had chosen surgery. In ninth grade I'd have to be put under to have my tonsils removed, and in tenth grade I'd shatter my nose during a softball game and have to be put under to have my nose repaired. As an adult I'd have several more surgeries, and to this day I haven't had a single weird reaction to the anesthetics. However, I'd be lying if I said that I don't get nervous before receiving anesthetics. No matter how hard I try to suppress the thoughts, I can't help but fear having some crazy reaction like the poor guy Mom told us about.

Croquet, Anyone?

The summer before Liz started her senior year was the summer Liz and Charlie began their infamous fights over boys. Being close in age and in the same small high school, their circles of friends were bound to overlap. Although their friends knew of one another's existence, they didn't intermingle—that is, not until this particular summer when Charlie decided to date Liz's best guy friend Steve. This did not go over well with hot-headed Liz.

Liz didn't want her little sister attending any of her senior parties, nor did she want her to hang out with her group of friends. She kept telling Charlie this was her senior year and to butt out of it! However, Charlie never liked being told what to do, so the more Liz told her to stay away from the senior crowd and not to date Steve, the more Charlie wanted to be involved in the senior crowd, and the more she wanted to date Steve. This led to Charlie and Liz constantly arguing over anything and everything. If Charlie ate the last Pop-Tart, Liz would scold her with "stop eating all the food," which would then turn into, "and while you're at it, stop dating my friends!"

As punishment for Liz and Charlie's constant bickering Mom ordered them to spend thirty minutes of daily peaceful time together until they could work out their differences. (Looking back, as I myself am now a mom of two girls, Mom's punishment was clever; however, after this particular summer day, Mom came to regret her choice of punishment.)

I had just come home from soccer practice. Immediately I headed downstairs to the kitchen to grab a Gatorade and make a

PB&J sandwich, my go-to snack after every practice. After making my sandwich, I walked from the kitchen into the adjoining family room and looked out the huge picture window overlooking the backyard.

As I ate my PB&J in front of the window, I was surprised to see Liz and Charlie playing what at first glance appeared to be a friendly game of croquet, and then I realized that they weren't playing out of love; they were just trying to get their "together time" out of the way. With this realization I laughed to myself and continued to watch the game unfold.

Since my sisters started high school they had outgrown tying me to chairs, locking me out on the roof, and torturing me throughout the summer. In order to let out their displaced aggression, they had turned to hitting things—such as balls—and croquet quickly became a favorite family pastime. Their game appeared to be close, and I had nothing better to do, so I stood and watched them through the window as I drank my lemon-lime Gatorade and ate my snack.

It was Charlie's turn. Liz was standing with one hand on her hip while she twirled her mallet like a flag with the other. Liz might not have been the athlete of the family, but she was darn good at twirling things. She was the only one of us girls to be on our high school's flag team, known as the color guard. I always liked watching Liz with her flag.

Charlie hit her green ball, and her smile widened as it went through a wicket, allowing her to take a bonus shot. From my view inside the house, Liz's ball looked too far ahead of Charlie's to be in danger of getting hit by Charlie's bonus shot. In the game, if your ball hits an opponent's, you are then allowed to hit your opponent's ball off course.

I watched Charlie squat down, close one eye, and extend her mallet out in front of her pointing it towards Liz's ball. I knew exactly what she was going to do—hit Liz's ball—but Liz's ball was too far away. I took a sip of my Gatorade and muttered to myself, "This ought to be good."

Even from inside the house, watching the game from afar, I could feel the tension lingering between my sisters. Whenever Charlie had an extra shot, she went for the kill, not the lead. I knew that, and so did Liz. Liz was now shaking her head, annoyed, watching as Charlie made her next move.

There's no way, Charlie, I chuckled to myself. *Liz's ball is too far away.* I shook my head as I watched Charlie take her shot.

Well, the impossible shot that seemed too far away wasn't impossible for all-star athlete Charlie McCoy. She hit her ball just far enough and hard enough to bounce and then roll and hit Liz's. Liz and I both stood there with our mouths wide open, stunned that Charlie had made that shot. But the events that took place after Charlie's next move were even more unpredictable.

Charlie joyfully skipped over to Liz's ball, set hers behind Liz's, placed her foot on her own ball, wound her mallet backwards, and smacked the crap out of Liz's. Liz's ball went so far off course that it hit our backyard fence. And with that, the game was over for Liz.

As Liz stared at her ball in disbelief, Charlie did a little victory dance. When it came to playing games with sisters, Charlie threw sportsmanship out the window.

Liz turned to see Charlie dancing with a smug look on her face. Words were exchanged between the two of them. Then without warning Liz charged Charlie, screaming and raising her mallet high above her head.

Dear God! I said to myself as my eyes widened in fear. *Liz is going to kill Charlie!* I stood there not knowing what to do as I watched the McCoy Croquet Rumble through the large picture window. I could hear Charlie's muffled laughing as Liz tackled her to the ground. Charlie's laughing only infuriated Liz even more. Liz sat on top of Charlie's stomach and then proceeded to smack her in the face, arms, and chest. Although everything was muffled through the glass, I knew Liz was screaming profanities.

Charlie stopped laughing at Liz momentarily then she knocked Liz off of her, stood up, and began to walk towards the house with a sly smirk on her face. But Liz wasn't done yet. She quickly jumped to her feet, grabbed her mallet, and began to chase after Charlie again. I'd be lying if I said I wasn't somewhat amused watching my sisters fight. For the first time in my life, I wasn't the one being chased, tackled, or punched. With that being said, I didn't know how to handle my sisters' recent fighting. There was no way I could intervene. Both of them were bigger than I was, and putting myself in the middle would only be subjecting myself to pain. Therefore, the only logical thing I could do was sit back and enjoy the show.

They were getting closer and closer to the house, and I could start to understand muffled bits and pieces of their conversation through the glass. Liz was mostly cursing Charlie and telling her how annoying she is while Charlie continued to laugh and say "whatever" to Liz. Liz continued to chase Charlie, but she wasn't as fast as her. Charlie continued to laugh as she slowed her stride to a brisk jog, as if she were taunting Liz, rubbing in the fact that she was faster. Liz's face was now bright red with anger. She knew she couldn't catch Charlie, so she threw her mallet with all her might towards Charlie, only to miss by a long shot. Charlie found this extremely funny—so funny that she stopped jogging to hold her stomach while she wiped tears of laughter from her face.

Beyond mad, Liz scrambled for any object within arm's reach. That's when the unimaginable happened. Liz grabbed Charlie's ball and threw it as hard as she could at Charlie's mocking face. For the first time in Liz's life, she had impeccable aim. Good thing Charlie was quick to react and lowered her head just in the nick of time. The ball went whizzing past Charlie's ducked head and was coming my way. I watched in disbelief as the ball hit the picture window directly in front of me, causing a loud cracking of glass.

Instinctively I dropped my Gatorade and PB&J, bent forward, and wrapped my arms tightly around my face and head to protect myself. As the huge window shattered all around me, my Gatorade hit the hard tile floor and then bounced back up, causing the sticky yellow liquid to splash up my legs. As the loud shattering of glass continued, I could feel little pieces of glass hit my body and land in my hair. I held my head and breath for what seemed like forever as the crashing of glass continued.

Once all the loud crackling and crashing of glass came to a halt, I slowly removed my arms from my head and fearfully opened my eyes. I was standing in a sticky pile of glass. In front of me, what once had been the huge window overlooking our backyard now contained no glass. I looked to my left and then to my right. Tiny specks of glass were everywhere in the family room and as far as I could see into the kitchen. My mouth dropped open as I looked at my sisters. I was speechless.

"Oh [BLEEP]!" Liz said as she began to pace in the yard. I could hear her as clear as day now.

"What were you thinking?" Charlie yelled at Liz. "Why the [BLEEP] would you throw a ball at the window?" Charlie scorned Liz as if she were a young child.

"Don't worry about me," I said to my sisters as I examined the damage they had just caused. I stood in a sticky mess of lemon-lime shards of glass. I patted my chest, arms, and legs looking for trickling blood or any signs of a cut, but luckily there was none. Little pieces of glass fell out of my hair and onto the floor as I bent over and continued to examine myself. "Really, guys," I yelled, "don't worry; I'm okay!" I added in a sarcastic tone, but my sisters continued to ignore me and went on with their arguing.

"I wasn't aiming for the window, Charlie," Liz defended herself, "I was aiming for your annoying face!" she screamed as she threw her arms in the air.

"Well, you have quite the aim," Charlie said in a sarcastic tone as she gave Liz a sly smile and pointed at the broken window.

"Sorry we can't all be as athletic as you are!" Liz yelled back.

"Enough!" I screamed as loudly as I possibly could at both of my sisters. They stopped fighting and looked at me stunned. They weren't used to me yelling at them. They knew I was mad. "If you haven't noticed, the back window is completely gone! Mom is going to kill us! And I'm standing in a huge pile of glass!" I gestured towards the floor surrounding me. I looked back at my sisters. They were both still in shock that I was yelling at them, so I decided to take this opportunity to let them have it.

"Liz," I screamed, "if Charlie hadn't moved, you would have shattered her face instead of the window! And Charlie, you won the stupid game, so please shut up already!" Not only were my sisters not used to me yelling at them but until this moment I had never pointed out their flaws.

Liz looked at Charlie, Charlie looked at Liz, and then they both looked at me.

"And I'm sick of you two constantly fighting!" I added in an even more annoyed tone. "So can the two of you please just shut up and get me out of this mess!" Although I was the youngest, at this moment I was the only one of us who was thinking clearly. A combination of my words and the fact that they had just broken the biggest window in our house managed to pull them both out of their hateful trance and focus on the problem at hand.

"Well [BLEEP]," Liz cursed, "let's get all this [BLEEP] cleaned up before Mom comes home and loses her [BLEEP]." Liz sighed then hung her head low in defeat as she slowly walked inside. Liz always cursed when she was mad or upset. Charlie followed.

Neither Liz nor Charlie spoke as they swept the floor. The only sound in the McCoy household was the clinking and clanking of pieces of glass being swept into a large pile. As they worked, I very carefully walked into the laundry room bathroom to undress. I stood in front of the sink and shook my head back and forth. Several pieces of glass fell out of my hair and into the sink. *Awesome!* I thought to myself. I knew I was most likely covered in small pieces of glass from head to toe. I knew I needed to get undressed and showered before accidentally getting hurt. The first clothing that needed to be taken off was my sticky cleats, soccer socks, and shin guards. As I pulled off my left shin guard, I immediately felt a sting and saw red blood pouring out from a thin long cut on the top of my shin. "Ouch!" I hissed as I removed the bloody piece of glass from my skin and threw it in the sink.

After several minutes of carefully removing all my clothing then shaking it into the sink to remove any glass, I managed to strip down to my sports bra and underwear with only a few cuts. I threw all my clothes into the washing machine, grabbed a dirty shirt of Mom's from off the laundry room floor, and put on her gardening boots. As I walked past my sisters to go upstairs to shower, neither one of them commented on my dress attire. They both glanced at me then continued to work in silence.

After showering and while getting dressed, I heard an unusual sound coming from downstairs—screaming. Unlike the angry screaming I had just witnessed between Liz and Charlie, this sounded like scared screaming. I ran down the steps as fast as I could only to witness a sight I had never seen before. "What the…" I said as I took in the scene.

Liz was standing on top of the barstool screeching like a terrified little girl, and Charlie was running back and forth between the family room and the kitchen swatting her broom every which way chasing after a squirrel! I shook my head to make sure that what I was seeing was really a live squirrel loose in our house, and then I sprang into action. I grabbed the other broom and joined Charlie in the squirrel chase.

"Get out! Get out of our house!" Charlie screamed at the squirrel as it leapt off the top of the refrigerator and down to the kitchen bar knocking over our fruit basket and causing fruit to go flying towards Liz and then onto the floor. The squirrel took off into the family room.

From on top of her barstool Liz stopped screaming and began cheering Charlie and me on as we chased after the squirrel. Until that moment I had never realized just how fast squirrels are or how far they could jump—or more like fly! Just when I thought the squirrel was going one way, it would switch directions leaving me tripping over my own feet while trying to mimic its agility. Or it would perch itself high on the family room shelving unit, knock down a couple of pictures, then squirrel-like fly over to the top of the kitchen cabinets. The squirrel was moving faster than Charlie or I could keep up. On several occasions we accidentally knocked into each other or swatted each other with our brooms.

After chasing the squirrel back and forth between the family room and kitchen for several minutes, the squirrel finally decided to exit through the recently broken window. Once it left, Liz began chanting as Charlie screamed, "Not in our house!" and I laughed. That squirrel adventure was just what the McCoy Boys needed. Before we did anything else, we found an old bed sheet and taped it over the broken back window to prevent any more unwelcome critters from entering our house. For the remainder of the day, the three of us laughed as we worked together to make sure we picked up every piece of glass. We found the smallest pieces of glass hiding in every inch of the lower level—the fireplace, the cracks between the floor tile, in the couch cushions… It was everywhere! We had to sweep and then vacuum and sweep and then vacuum again and again until we couldn't find any more glass.

After we finally finished cleaning, we entertained ourselves by doing live reenactments of us chasing after the rogue squirrel. I watched from on top of the barstool and pretended to be Liz while Charlie and Liz pretended to chase the squirrel. We all switched roles and continued to pretend our ninja skills were why the squirrel decided to leave, when really we knew we had been completely at the mercy of the squirrel.

As we laughed, I looked at my sisters and shook my head. Just an hour ago, Liz was trying to kill Charlie, and now we were laughing about the wild squirrel chase. Ah, sisters! After we had our fun with the squirrel, we laughed over the agonizing fact that for the first time in Liz's life, not only did she have good aim but she threw a ball hard enough to shatter a six-foot window. Oh, the irony! Before we knew it, it was time for Mom to come home, and we all sat on the upstairs living room couch dreading her walking through the front door.

"You can date Steve," Liz said as we anxiously waited, "on two conditions: one, you ask me before coming to any of the senior parties; and two, Friday night football game hangouts are off limits!"

"Well, Liz, after today, I have a feeling neither one of us will be attending any senior parties," Charlie sighed then added, "but okay, if Mom doesn't kill us or ground us for life, we have a deal," she said as she shook Liz's hand.

I let out a huge sigh of relief. I knew this wouldn't be the last argument between Liz and Charlie over boys or parties, but I knew this was what Mom had been waiting for—for them to come to some kind of agreement on their own. We heard the keys in the lock, and I braced myself for what was about to come.

"Welcome home, our beautiful, loving mother!" Charlie said in her best sweet and innocent voice.

"Have we told you how much we love you?" Liz added as she batted her eyes.

"Dear God," Mom said as she threw her purse down on the armchair and placed her hands on her hips. Then with raised eyebrows and flushed cheeks she asked, "What have you girls done now?"

Mom was a smart woman, and she knew that if all three of us were awaiting her arrival and buttering her up with compliments as soon she walked through the door, it meant one thing and one thing only: we had done something terribly wrong. Needless to say, after we explained what had happened and showed Mom the back window, she was very, very unhappy with all three of us—so unhappy that she didn't even crack a smile when we told her about how we had to defend our home against a squirrel.

I got off easily. I was grounded for a week; whereas, Liz and Charlie were grounded until further notice and had to pay to replace the broken window. It doesn't quite seem fair that I got grounded when I was literally the innocent bystander, but I have learned that when you're the youngest child, no matter what you did or didn't do, something is always your fault. I've also learned that when you're the youngest, you can blame things that you are guilty of on your older siblings, so it probably all evens out in the end.

Throughout Liz's senior year, she and Charlie had several more disagreements over boys and parties; however, they never brought down another window. One fight did, however, result in Charlie giving Liz a bloody nose. But that's another story.

My Very Own Space

I'll never forget the mixed emotions I felt when Liz graduated from high school and left for college at The University of Cincinnati. It all seemed to happen so quickly—taking pictures at her senior prom, watching her throw her graduation cap, eating cake at her party, helping her pack up her room . . . And then, before I knew it, moving day was upon us, and Mom and Dad were helping her move into her sorority house leaving her bedroom empty and up for grabs!

It was the August before I started the eighth grade, and for the first time in my fourteen years of existence, I would have my very own room. After all those years of sharing every single inch of my room with Charlie, I would finally get to experience what it is like to have my own space. There would be no more fights between Charlie and me over dividing our room into fair segments (with Charlie always getting a bigger portion than me. On several occasions Charlie went so far as to duct tape our floor in order to keep me off of her side and out of her stuff.) I would have an entire room all to myself to fill with my own bed, my own dresser and my own desk. I could decorate the entire room with posters of my own choosing. I could listen to my music as loud as I wanted without Charlie complaining and telling me to turn it down. Mom may have been upset to see her oldest daughter leave the nest, but Charlie and I were on cloud nine.

As Mom and I set up my new room, I couldn't believe how much space I had. The first couple of weeks were amazing. I could jump into my bed without finding a random dirty sock, bra—or worse, Charlie's dirty underwear—lying there. When I opened my closet, Charlie's clothes were no longer overtaking my side. I could turn the lights out whenever I wanted, and I didn't have to listen to Charlie sneaking the phone into our room after "lights out" so she could gossip quietly with her crew. I could sit on my bed and write notes to my friends without having to worry about Charlie stealing them from me only to read them and make fun of me. At the age of fourteen, I was experiencing what it felt like to have privacy and space of my own. And so was Charlie. We were both loving the new arrangement.

Then August came to an end, and so did my summer. School started, and all the changes began to sink in. When Liz lived at home, the mornings had been full of chaos. While getting ready for school, Charlie would play Weezer while across the hall Liz would blare her beloved Garth Brooks. Some days I'd go to school with a headache feeling as if I had just left a weird country-punk concert. Now without Liz at home, there were no more music wars while getting ready, and no more Mom yelling at us girls to turn down the ruckus.

Even the car rides to school were different. When Liz drove us to school, I'd sit in the back seat and listen to her and Charlie gossip over who was dating whom and all the latest school drama. But now Charlie and I sat quietly in the back seat as Mom sang along to her oldies and drove us to school. Liz's absence was beginning to sink in. I wondered how the drive to school would be once Charlie had her license. I couldn't see her gossiping with me as she had with Liz.

After several weeks of adjusting to our new morning routine, being back at school, and having our own rooms, the mornings began to seem a little too quiet, and my room began to feel a little too big and—dare I say it—a little lonely. Oddly enough, I began to miss lying in bed trying to fall asleep while Charlie teased me about my "stupid friends" and my "stupid life." Lying in my quiet, big room, I realized that I wouldn't mind telling Charlie about the latest cheer drama even though I knew she'd just laugh at me. I knew her laughing at me was her way of finding things amusing.

As I lay in bed trying to sleep, I looked around and thought back on how this room used to be the room where I'd run to hide from Charlie. This is the room where I'd come when I was seeking advice on all things girl related, where I learned how to paint my nails and do my hair. This is the room where I'd come to vent if I'd had a bad day, or to complain about Mom and Dad. It's where I watched Liz get ready for all her dances and where she grew up. I realized that although I had changed the decor and the paint on the walls, every inch of this room was filled with a memory of Liz—and I began to cry. This room would always be Liz's—never truly mine. I had been so excited about having my own room that I had overlooked the more important fact that Liz had moved out. That night, I realized how much I missed Liz and that she was never moving back, and in that moment I knew that I would easily give up having my own room if it meant having Liz back home.

Although Charlie wouldn't admit it, I think in her own way she missed having her annoying little sister around and missed having Liz at home as well. One night after dinner, while sitting on my bed doing my homework, Charlie slowly walked past my door only to backtrack and lean up against its frame.

"Whatcha doing, dork?" she asked.

"Homework," I said without looking up from my math book.

"Lame!" she said as she invited herself in and plopped herself down onto my bed by my feet.

I pretended to ignore her, although I couldn't help but secretly smile to myself. From what I could tell, Charlie was taking an interest in me without being forced to by Mom!

"Ugh," she moaned. "I hated Mrs. Cromer's math class," Charlie said as she flipped through my math binder sitting next to her, "and," she added as she sniffed the air around my feet, "your feet stiinnnkk!"

"They do not!" I protested as I threw my math book to the side and gave Charlie a swift kick in the arm.

My kick didn't even faze her; she just laughed at me. "Speaking of feet," Charlie began, "remember when Liz and I used to hold you down and dangle Dad's dirty socks in your face?" She chuckled.

"Ugh!" I moaned then pinched my nose shut as if the smell could travel through time. "How could I forget?" I said as I tried not to think of the disgusting smell of his stinky socks. "Seriously, his socks made me puke!" I couldn't help it; the memories were too realistic. I gagged a little then swallowed hard to keep from puking.

Charlie chuckled. "Okay, drama queen," she said as she swatted my hand from my nose and rolled her eyes indicating that I was overreacting. Then her laughing subsided and her tone changed as she added, "But about that . . . Liz and I found out that Dad had some kind of foot infection," she looked at me with apologetic eyes. "That's why his socks smelled so bad. Liz—and I (she faintly added)—felt awful for dangling those dirty, germ-infested socks in your face all those times!"

"Is that why you stopped?" I asked horrified. I could literally picture thousands of germs laughing at me as they jumped off of Dad's socks and onto my face.

"Yup," Charlie shamefully admitted.

"Oh, my goodness! Thank God you didn't put those things in my mouth!" I said as I grabbed my pillow from behind my back and flung it at her face. "And you wonder why I'm such a germ freak with my two sisters constantly doing crap like that?!"

Charlie just shrugged and laughed.

As our laughing subsided, I looked around my room and again I couldn't help but miss Liz. "You think Liz likes living in her sorority house?" I asked, my voice filled with sadness.

"I don't know," Charlie shrugged. I could tell she had been thinking of Liz just as much as I had been.

Charlie smirked and jokingly said, "You'd think after living in our crazy house with us crazy girls, Liz wouldn't want to move into a bigger house full of even more crazy girls," and then forced a laugh. I could tell Charlie was trying to make a joke, but there was sadness in her eyes. Sadness was an emotion Charlie hardly ever showed. "Anyway," she said obviously trying to change the subject, "what's new with your stupid friends? Got a new lame boyfriend?" she asked with a smile.

That night was the first time Charlie and I sat on my bed and talked like I had heard normal sisters do, and something between us began to change.

* * *

The following week when Liz came home for Sunday night dinner with three huge bags of laundry, she quickly recruited her little sisters to help carry in all her stuff. As I eagerly ran to her car to greet her with a longing hug, Charlie walked coolly behind me and greeted Liz with a loving pat on the shoulder then helped Liz lug her stuff inside. Had this been two months ago, Charlie would have been too busy with her own life and told Liz to carry her own stuff; however, that night both Charlie and I were more than willing to help her. It felt like forever since Liz had been home.

As Liz sorted through her laundry, she excitedly told us all about college life. Charlie sat on top of the dryer as I stood leaning against the doorway listening enviously and trying to hold back tears. Liz seemed so happy. I feared that after tonight she'd leave home and wouldn't come back until Thanksgiving—or worse, Christmas! She beamed as she told us how amazing it felt to have the freedom she'd been dreaming of for years.

"The best part," she added as she poured the laundry detergent into the washer, "is that I don't have to follow any of Mom's ridiculous rules—no curfew, no controlling who I hang out with; I can go wherever I want, whenever I want!"

"Sounds amazing." Charlie was grinning ear to ear. "Won't be too much longer until it's my turn!" she beamed enviously.

"Oh Charlie, I forgot to mention one of the best parts of college—hot boys everywhere!" Liz laughed.

"Finally!" Charlie laughed along with her. "Slim pickin's in Deer Park!" she chuckled.

As they joked and laughed and talked about college parties, I couldn't help but feel sick as a giant knot in my stomach began to tighten. Charlie was right. In two years it would be her turn to leave our childhood home on Glenbury Lane, and then what would I do? With both of my sisters gone away to college, that would leave Mom and me alone in the house. If I thought my room felt big and empty now, I couldn't imagine how the entire house would feel after both Liz and Charlie were gone!

Liz looked over to me. I knew my face was pained sad with concern. Things were changing faster than I wanted them to, and I didn't like it. I didn't bother trying to hide my feelings from Liz; she knew me far too well. Throughout the years she had protected me from the wrath of Charlie and comforted me when I needed it. She took one look at me and knew how I was feeling.

She finished putting her laundry in the washer then shut the lid. This time when she spoke, less excitement filled her voice. "I mean college is awesome overall, but it's not all fun and games. It sucks to have to pay for everything, and I mean everything, Charlie—all your books, your rent, your parking space, your meals and snacks, even every Coke I drink…" Her sentence began to trail as she shrugged her shoulders. "When I think back to living at home, it wasn't so bad here. Sure, Mom and Dad made us work to have spending money, but now that I have to pay for everything on my own, I feel like I'm constantly working. Today's my first day off since I've been gone." She walked towards me, leaned against the other side of the door, and gently patted my back. "Why do you think I haven't been home to visit yet?" she asked as she gave me a loving smile. "I seriously haven't had the time!"

I gave a sad understanding nod. Knowing that Liz hadn't come home yet to visit because she hadn't had the time made me feel a little better, but I missed her—and Charlie practically had one foot out the door! Charlie could be a royal pain in my ass, but I wasn't ready to lose both of my sisters. I sighed and tried to remind myself that at least for now Charlie is stuck at home.

"I've been going to class then working every day, and on weekends I'm studying and trying keep up with all the crazy college coursework," Liz said as she gave my shoulder a loving squeeze. She looked back towards Charlie and said, "You have it good here, Charlie. I know we all can drive each other nuts, but once you move away from all the craziness, you end up kind of missing it," she said as she let out a small laugh. "Mom's rules are absolutely ridiculous," Liz said as she rolled her eyes, "but you guys have it good. I'm starting to understand what Apple means when she tells us to enjoy high school because after you graduate, life comes at you fast and hard. College is hard! But you two nerdy brainiacs won't have to worry about that." Liz playfully rubbed her hand on the top of my head making my hair a mess. I couldn't help but smile.

Even though Liz had only been gone for a month, she had changed, and things at home were changing too. Charlie's look of envy slowly began to fade as she realized Liz had some good points that she hadn't thought of. Sure, college life may bring the freedom Charlie was anxiously dreaming of, but she hadn't realized that freedom comes with the price of many new responsibilities that she wasn't looking forward to.

Liz continued, "Just try to take Apple's advice and enjoy the free ride while it lasts. Okay, enough of this life lesson crap. Let's eat; I'm starved!" she said as she pulled me in for a hug and whispered into my ear, "Love ya, kiddo."

Growing up, Liz always looked out for me. In fact there were times when I called her mini-mommy. Throughout the years she had protected me from Charlie, listened to me whenever I had a problem, and comforted me when I was down. Whenever I needed her, she was always there for me. I hadn't realized how much I depended on Liz until she wasn't across the hall from me anymore. Funny thing about life—sometimes you don't realize how good you have things until things change, and you don't have that someone or something anymore.

When Liz left that night to go back to her new home, a void instantly filled our home. As Charlie, Mom, and I sat on the couch quietly watching Sunday night TV, I could tell they felt the void as much as I did. Then to my surprise, Charlie nudged me—bringing me out of my missing-Liz trance—and passed me the bowl of popcorn. I was shocked! Normally Charlie went to great lengths to keep her food all to herself. Knowing I'm a germ freak, there were times she'd cough on or lick her food, or even go so far as to spit a loogie in her snack, just to avoid having to share with me. However, that night Charlie offered to share. I gratefully took a handful then passed the bowl back. As I ate the popcorn, I realized that not only had things changed in the McCoy household but the McCoy Boys were changing too.

Flash the Wonder Fish

The leaves had turned an autumn red-orange and fallen from the trees, and a cool chill filled the air. My favorite Cincinnati weather had arrived. It was now cool enough to wear a sweatshirt and jeans all day long. My Friday nights were spent watching Charlie cheer on our losing high school football team, and my weekends were consumed with soccer games and bonfires with my friends. What made this fall special? Well, this was the first year I would be marching in our homecoming parade with the cheerleading squad. Normally Charlie would be marching with the cheer squad as well; however, she had a more important role. This year, Charlie was a homecoming court candidate! Charlie sat perched on the back of Aunt Anne's little red convertible wearing a homecoming court sash and waving to the cheering crowd. Occasionally Charlie would take a break from waving to throw candy to the little kids who lined the curb.

Liz came home to watch with Mom and Dad as I marched and Charlie smiled, waved, and yelled McCoy for homecoming queen!

The parade ended at our high school, and everyone headed to the football stadium to watch the homecoming football game. I sat with my friends in the student section and watched Liz cheer until halftime then I eagerly joined Mom, Dad, and Liz in the stands to watch the halftime show. Tonight, instead of our marching band performing, the announcer was introducing the homecoming court candidates one by one. When we heard "Charlie McCoy" echo throughout the stadium from the loudspeakers, we stood and cheered for her proudly. Charlie smiled and waved to the cheering crowd as she pranced down the fifty yard line in her cheer uniform. As she joined the rest of the candidates on the track, she gave a little curtsy and blew kisses to her friends in the stands. Charlie loved to be the center of attention, and that night, with the stadium's huge fluorescent lights shining down on her, she literally was in the spotlight. Mom and Dad couldn't have been more proud. They couldn't help but boast to everyone sitting around us: "That's our daughter!" After halftime, I joined my friends again to watch our team lose. Although our team didn't pull off a win that night, seeing Charlie so happy was a win in my family's eyes.

The next day was the homecoming dance. When I woke up and headed down to grab some breakfast, I was surprised to see that overnight our kitchen bar had transformed into a mini salon. The table was covered with nail polish, makeup, hot rollers, a hair dryer, hairspray, and more beauty products than I never knew existed. Liz had always been the girly girl of us McCoys; whereas, Charlie and I were more the tomboys. While I spent my free time in the backyard perfecting soccer moves, Liz spent her down time tanning and painting her nails. Her nails always looked as if she had just stepped out of the salon, and she could spend hours perfecting her hair and makeup. My nails were always chewed down to nothing, and my idea of putting on makeup was slapping on my favorite flavor of Lip Smackers.

As I examined the McCoy mini salon, I realized that all of the products lying on the table Liz had brought over to use on our potential homecoming queen to get her ready for her big dance tonight. I laughed and thought to myself, *This ought to be good!* When it came to makeup, Charlie was just as clueless as I was. Unfortunately, I was going to miss half of the afternoon due to a double-header soccer game, but I knew that when I returned home, I was in for a treat. I continued to smile and laugh as I made myself some peanut butter toast and orange juice then got ready for my games.

Hours later, I returned home exhausted from soccer but ready to see what my sisters had been up to. Dad gave me a quick kiss on the forehead and told me he'd be back later tonight to see Charlie before she left for the dance, and I eagerly jumped out of his truck. Upon entering the house, I immediately heard yelling coming from the kitchen.

"I look like a clown, Liz!" Charlie screamed.

I smiled as I ran my bag up to my room and then raced downstairs to witness what I was sure was going to be an epic McCoy Boy argument!

"You look amazing!" Liz was telling Charlie as I entered the kitchen. "You're just not used to wearing makeup. You're used to looking like a scrub, so it's going to take some getting used to!" Liz sassed.

"Liz, if you're going to make me look like a complete fool then I don't want your frickin' help!" Charlie said as she picked up a makeup remover pad and began to wipe off all the makeup I'm sure Liz had just spent an hour doing.

"Stop that!" Liz instructed. "It looks good!" she reassured Charlie as she anxiously tried to grab the makeup remover pad from Charlie's hand.

"It's too much!" Charlie scorned as she swatted Liz away and continued to furiously scrub off her eye makeup.

"Ugh! Why do you have to be so impossible?!" Liz groaned as she threw her hands up in the air giving in to Charlie's stubbornness.

"Well, hi there, sisters!" I said cheerfully as I grabbed a bottled water out of the fridge.

"I won both of my soccer games, in case you were wondering!" I said proudly.

"Well, you look like a rat and smell like a boys' locker room!" Charlie snapped.

"Good job, Em!" Liz congratulated me. "I'd hug you, but Charlie's right—you smell awful!" she said playfully.

I stuck my tongue out at the two of them and said, "Well, Charlie, you're in a good mood!"

"I look like crap, and Neil will be here in a couple of hours for pictures," she said as she continued to wipe all the makeup off her face.

"Her makeup looked amazing!" Liz said as she rolled her eyes. "I think something else is bothering her," Liz said with a sly smile.

Instantly I was intrigued. Nothing really bothered Charlie. Growing up, she wasn't afraid of anything and never showed any signs of weakness.

"Oh really…" I said to Liz as I sat down on the barstool next to Charlie.

Charlie glared at Liz then looked at me. "Nothing is bothering me!" she snapped. "And for real, Em, you stink! Go shower and then make yourself useful! Grab my dress and bring it down here," she instructed.

I just stared at her willing her to ask nicely.

She rolled her eyes, "Please, already!" she said as she gently nudged me off my chair to get me moving.

"Fine!" I said as I put my water down on the table. "Where's Mom?" I asked as I looked around the family room. I hadn't seen or heard her since I walked in the door.

"She's picking up lunch and Neil's boutonniere," Liz answered. "She should be back soon."

I nodded my head. "So Liz, what do you think is bothering Charlie?" I asked.

Before I could move, Charlie turned and gave me a swift punch in the bicep. "Ouch!" I screamed as I rubbed my arm.

"Really, Charlie?" Liz said.

I didn't want to stick around and risk getting abused any longer, so I left the wicked homecoming queen and her makeup peasant in the McCoy Salon and went upstairs to shower. After showering and getting dressed, I went into Charlie's room to bring down her jewelry, dress, and the shoes she had laid out. I knew I didn't have to, especially after she bruised my arm, but I didn't want to upset her any more than she already was. This was an important night for her.

I looked around Charlie's room and couldn't help but notice all the trophies, ribbons, and awards. Charlie was good at everything she had ever tried. That's when it occurred to me that Charlie doesn't take losing well. I think the one time I beat her at Candy Land, she folded up the board and proceeded to use it to smack me on the head, but I didn't care. As strong as Charlie was, the board didn't hurt, so I curled up in a ball and continued to laugh hysterically, ecstatic that I had finally beat Charlie at a game.

Tonight Charlie was a player in a new game—a game she had never played before—a popularity game. Whoever received the most votes would be named homecoming queen, and she had no control over who her classmates voted for. For the first time in Charlie's life, whether she won or lost was out of her control. This wasn't soccer. She couldn't try to make the winning goal to pull the team to victory. Or softball, where it was up to her to hit the winning homerun as she had done several times in the past. No, there was nothing she could physically do. All she could do was smile, wave, and be nice to her classmates and hope they like her enough to vote for her. Not to mention, if she did lose, she wouldn't be losing in front of a small crowd; she'd be losing in front of all her friends and classmates. I now knew what Liz had already figured out.

I grabbed her dress off her bed and quickly turned to head downstairs. As I turned, my hip hit the corner of her nightstand causing it to shake and sending a shooting pain through my hip. I yelped as I sat down on her bed and rubbed my hip willing it to stop hurting. First my arm and now my hip; I was going to be a bruised mess! After sitting for a couple of minutes, the pain subsided. When I stood up, I realized that when my hip knocked into the nightstand, water had spilled out of Flash the Wonder Fish's fish bowl, and a small puddle had formed on the floor. Flash the Wonder Fish was Charlie's newest pet. Her boyfriend Neil had won it for her at the end of the summer at our church's festival. Charlie loved that stupid fish more than I had ever seen her care about anything, so I couldn't let anything happen to it. I set Charlie's dress back down, cleaned up the spilled water, and picked up the fish bowl to refill it. In the bathroom I turned on room temperature water and filled his bowl back up then very carefully walked him back into Charlie's room, set him on the nightstand, and sprinkled some fish food into his bowl.

"There ya go, Flash," I said. "Good as new." I grabbed Charlie's dress, shoes, and jewelry then wobbled down the stairs to rejoin my sisters soccer-stench free.

This time upon entering the kitchen, the scene had changed from sisterly bickering to Mom and daughters laughing. From the looks of it, Liz had re-applied Charlie's makeup, and since Charlie wasn't complaining, I assumed she was happy with it. Her hair was up in a curly, messy bun. As she sat there in her white robe laughing about something with Mom and Liz, I couldn't help but think that she looked like royalty.

"Hey, Em!" Mom greeted me with a kiss on the forehead. We would have hugged, but my arms were full.

"Hey, Mom!" I smiled as I walked over to Charlie and threw down her heels next to her barstool.

"Dad said you played well!" Mom beamed proudly. "Sorry I had to miss your games, but I needed to be here to help get everything ready for tonight," she said apologetically.

"It's okay," I reassured her as I placed Charlie's jewelry down on the table next to her and said, "I don't think you've ever missed a game, Mom. I understand." Mom was the best at being at everything we girls did—school concerts, cheerleading, track and field, soccer, softball... It didn't matter what was the event; Mom was there.

"Got you a sandwich; it's in the fridge," Mom said.

"Thanks, Mom!" I smiled then asked Charlie, "Is this everything you need, Queen?" as I held up her dress.

Charlie looked at the jewelry and shoes and then snatched her dress from my hands.

"That'll do, peasant!" she said in a snotty voice as she raised her hand and shooed me away. She got up from the stool to hang her dress on the laundry room's bathroom door. She returned to her prepping station and held up her shoes. "Liz, what do you think about these?" she asked.

"Eh, they're alright. I brought you some other shoes and jewelry to choose from; they're in a bag next to your bed." Liz smiled back at her.

"Thanks!" Charlie smiled. "I'll go grab them," she said.

"Who are you, and what have you done with Charlie?" I laughed as I grabbed my sandwich out of the fridge.

"Sisters, sisters, there were never such devoted sisters," Mom began to sing. This was something she and Apple did whenever we were picking on one another to divert us from a huge argument.

"Em's right, Mom. You should have seen her thirty minutes ago. She was a little...stressed," Liz said.

"Whatever!" Charlie snapped. "You two just don't know how stressful it is to be Queen. There's so much pressure to be perfect!" Charlie sighed.

"You're not Queen yet!" I pointed out. "What happens if you lose?" I playfully teased. However, Charlie didn't take it so playfully, and instantly I could see the fear growing in her eyes.

"Em!" Mom snapped as Charlie just stood there in her place.

"You're not going to lose!" Liz said reassuringly to Charlie. "I mean, you're Charlie McCoy. You never lose at anything," Liz said reassuringly as she walked over and hugged her.

So there you have it. After years and years of feeling as if I was always the vulnerable one, I realized that Charlie had a weakness as well: she was afraid to lose.

"Easy for you guys to say! Neither of you has ever been the center of attention in front of the whole school with all eyes on you." Charlie rolled her eyes at us.

"Sure I have," Liz said. "Don't you remember my senior-year flag solo?" Liz reminded Charlie.

"Well, what I meant is that all my friends are expecting me to win. If I don't, it will be absolutely humiliating in front of the entire school." Charlie confessed.

"Or a life lesson," Liz said. "You can't win at everything, Charlie. Eventually at some point in your life, you will lose at something," Liz said sympathetically.

"This is true, Charlie dear," Mom said as she approached Charlie and lovingly gave her a reassuring hug. "You are an amazing daughter and person, but there will come a time in your life when you will lose at something. It happens to everyone. Losing homecoming court wouldn't be the worst thing that could happen. And besides, there's always prom court next year!" Mom tried to reassure her.

Charlie's eyes lit up. "You're right, Mom!" Charlie said. "Being prom queen would be better—so much better—than winning homecoming queen!" Charlie agreed.

At our school, homecoming court was for juniors, and prom court was for seniors. The prom king and queen had a special part in graduation and were invited back the following year to crown their successors. Instantly Charlie wasn't so concerned about homecoming court, and she was focused on winning prom queen a year from now.

Mom just laughed and sighed. "Oh, Charlie, you never fail to amuse me." Then she looked at Liz and me. "I'm going to run to the store to buy some film for the camera," then she looked back at Charlie and added, "Try not to kill one another while I'm gone!" then left out the back door.

"Okay, servants, time to make me look fabulous!" Charlie said as she ran up to her room to grab Liz's jewelry and heels.

As soon as she left, I shook my head and looked at Liz. She just shrugged her shoulders and sighed. Just as I took a bite of my sandwich, there was a loud thud, and the ceiling above Liz and me shook as Charlie began to scream.

"What the—" Liz said as she and ran upstairs to see what was the matter. I tossed my sandwich down on the table and followed close behind her.

As Liz and I turned the corner of Charlie's room, we witnessed a confusing and strange sight— Charlie hopping around on one foot while sobbing hysterically causing her mascara to run down her cheeks leaving black lines and ruining her perfect makeup. Neither Liz nor I had ever witnessed Charlie in such a state. We quickly moved to one side of the hallway to get out of her way as she hopped past us and into the bathroom.

"What's wrong?" Liz frantically asked as Charlie hopped by.

"Get out of my way!" Charlie sobbed as she pushed me against the hallway wall.

"What did I do?!" I confusedly asked unaware of what I had done to upset and possibly injure Charlie. And why was she hopping on one foot?

"You're a murderer!" she screamed at me as she entered the bathroom, sat down on the edge of the bathtub, and held up her right foot for us to see what she was so upset about. On the bottom of Charlie's foot was a horrid sight—Flash the Wonder Fish—or what used to be Flash. The fish was now dead, smashed and stuck to the bottom of Charlie's foot. Poor Flash's insides were coming out from all angles of his flattened body.

Liz and I both gasped in horror.

"Don't just stand there!" Charlie cried. "Get him off of me!" she ordered.

I took one look at Liz and knew she wasn't going to be of any help. Sure, Liz could handle watching blood and guts on her favorite TV show, ER, but when it came to real-life blood and guts—even a fish's—Liz couldn't handle it. Luckily for Charlie, years of chasing me with worms, spiders, and garden snakes had prepared me for this precise moment.

I pushed Liz out of the way, flung open the toilet seat, grabbed some toilet paper, and in one swift motion grabbed poor Flash's squished body from the bottom of Charlie's foot. I wrapped him in the toilet paper, gently placed him in the toilet, and quickly closed the lid.

As Liz wiped the mascara streaks from Charlie's face with a tissue and gave her another one to blow her nose with, I used soap and water to scrub all the fish guts off of Charlie's foot.

As I washed her foot, Charlie angrily cried, "You were the last one in my room!" and then added, "What did you do to him?" and threw her snotty tissue at me.

I had never seen Charlie break down like this over anything before. I knew she was going to hate me no matter what I said.

"I accidentally knocked some water out," I paused, "so I added some more," I shamefully admitted. "I was just trying to help."

"Well, you did help, Em; you helped kill him!" she screamed. I could see the anger growing in her eyes. "And now Neil will be here soon, and he'll think that I killed our pet!" Charlie growled.

I knew I had to fix this situation, and I had to fix it fast. "I'm sorry!" I pleaded as I patted her foot dry. "I'm going to make it up to you," I said as I stood up and ran out of the bathroom and into my room.

"You can't fix this!" Charlie yelled from the bathroom. But I wasn't listening to her. I had already grabbed my purse, dumped all its contents onto my bed, and shoved some money into my pocket as I ran down the stairs and out the back door. Outside I grabbed my bike and helmet then took off as fast as my legs could pedal. I knew I had to get to the pet store and back before Neil arrived at our house. I pedaled up Wicklow Hill, the highest hill in our neighborhood, in record-breaking time only to fly down faster than I thought was possible. I was terrified of wrecking my bike but more terrified of what Charlie would do to me if Neil found out that I killed their pet fish. After surviving the hill, I pedaled two more blocks to our local shopping center. As I passed our IGA, I slowed my pace so I wouldn't crash into anyone walking on the sidewalk. I let out a sigh of relief when I saw that Mom's van was still parked outside the store. I knew I still had time. I passed several more stores and finally arrived at the pet store. I jumped off my bike, threw it to the ground, and breathlessly ran in to the store.

"Excuse me," I panted, "but I need to buy a goldfish—and fast…please." I tried to catch my breath as I followed the worker over to the fish tanks. I pointed to a goldfish that looked to be about the same size that Flash was. The guy working at the pet store used a net to scoop up the goldfish and placed it in a plastic bag with water and food then tied the bag shut with a twist tie. After I paid, I very gently put the plastic bag containing the new

Flash inside my purse. I hung my purse over my neck and adjusted the strap so it would rest on my chest so I could keep my eye on the fish while riding home. I jumped on my bike and, more carefully this time, began to pedal home.

When I arrived home, Charlie and Neil were in the front yard, and Mom was taking pictures while Dad stood off to the side next to Liz taking it all in. Even from afar, I could tell that Charlie was forcing herself to smile. I was careful to ride my bike up the driveway behind the van so Charlie and Neil wouldn't be able to see what I was carrying. I parked my bike on the back porch and ran inside and up to Charlie's bedroom. Before putting the new Flash the Wonder Fish into his bowl, I made sure to dump some of the water out. After I had safely transferred the fish into the bowl, I very carefully carried it outside to Charlie.

"I thought you might want a picture with Flash!" I smiled as I handed the bowl to Charlie.

I noticed Charlie's makeup had been reapplied and her hair had been fixed. She was wearing Liz's dangling silver earrings and sparkly heels. I had to admit, the silver looked great up against her fitted black dress, and Liz had done an amazing job on her hair and makeup. She looked beautiful—like a queen.

As I approached her, her smile faded, and I couldn't tell if she was going to punch me or take the bowl from me. Then Neil said, "Great idea, Em," and took the bowl from Charlie and said, "Hey there, Flash!" and smiled. With that, Charlie beamed, and her fake smile was finally replaced with a genuine one. Luckily for me, goldfish all look alike, and Neil couldn't tell that the fish in the bowl wasn't the original Flash.

I stood off to the side with Liz and Dad and watched Mom continue to take picture after picture of the happy couple with their pet fish. Before we knew it, it was time for the royal couple to leave for dinner and then the dance. We all wished them luck on court then hugged Charlie goodbye. As they pulled away, Liz put her arm around me. "Ya did good, kid," she said as she smiled and hugged me.

That night, neither Liz nor I could find it in ourselves to eat the tuna noodle casserole Mom had made for dinner. We couldn't get the images of poor flattened Flash out of our minds. We waited until Mom had finished eating dinner to fill her in on the Flash drama that had occurred while she ran to the store. Mom ordered a pizza for Liz and me and threw out the remaining tuna noodle casserole instead of saving the leftovers for later.

Liz and I fell asleep on the couch watching TV while we waited for Charlie to return home. Although I wouldn't admit it, I wanted to hear all about the dance. Around one thirty, I woke up to Charlie shaking me. I rubbed my eyes as she shrieked, "Wake up, peasants! Your queen has returned home!" she exclaimed as she waved a silver crown in my face. Liz and I both sat up and started to scream in excitement.

"I knew you'd win!" Liz said tiredly but proudly.

"Were you surprised?" I asked Charlie.

"No," Charlie said confidently.

Liz and I took turns trying on the queen's crown as she told us all about how amazing it felt to be crowned queen in front of her friends and classmates.

"When the king and I took the floor for our dance, everyone was watching, and it felt like time stood still," she said as she snatched the crown from off my head. She put the crown back on and continued to brag. "It felt like a movie." She smiled as she danced around the living room floor. "And I was the star!"

And there we sat on the couch—three sisters (one queen and two commoners)—laughing and talking as Charlie reminisced on her evening. That night, Charlie was a star in more than just her family's eyes.

The Roof, the Roof, the Roof is—!

Nothing beats the feeling of walking out of school on the last day—the feeling of knowing you have two months of no homework, no tests, and no stress until the fall. And this year, as the bell rang and my friends and I walked out the school doors, we weren't leaving only to start summer break; we were walking out of junior high for the very last time. Next year when we returned, instead of walking in through the back doors that led to the junior high level of the building, we'd enter through the front school doors, which led to the second floor—the high school level. Yes, that's right—I, Emily K. McCoy, was now in ninth grade and an official high school student. This called for celebration!

Caroline, Sam, Nina, Lucy, Bailey, and I all headed to my house to grab some lunch before going to the pool. Normally we all hung out at Caroline's or Lucy's house because they had a finished basement with a TV and a mini-fridge, but not today. Today I was not only excited to be a high schooler but I was excited to show off my new-to-me trampoline!

One of Mom's friend's children had outgrown her trampoline, so she decided to pass it down to me! The springs were a little rusted, and the trampoline would only last a few more years, but I didn't care. I had always wanted a trampoline, and now my dream had come true—not to mention, it had come at the perfect time—the last week of school. Mom helped me set it up just in time to enjoy it all summer long with my friends. Charlie was a little annoyed that she had always wanted a trampoline and had never got one, but she understood that in one short year, she'd be off to college. Anyway, she was too busy juggling a part-time job, cheerleading, playing softball, and hanging with her far-too-cool-to-be-associated-with-me friends to use a trampoline.

After the pizza arrived, my friends and I headed out to the trampoline with pizza, chips, and soda pop in hand. As we sat on the trampoline eating and talking, summer excitement filled the air. I couldn't help but think to myself that this was *my* summer. Not only was this the summer leading up to high school but I was the only one of my friends who owned a trampoline. This summer, my house would be the place to hang out.

Little did I know, as Charlie was on her way home, she was having similar thoughts. In her mind, this was *her* summer—the summer before she started her senior year. To her, this was the summer of Charlie.

My friends and my "summer bucket list" conversation and lunch were suddenly interrupted by Charlie and her friends.

"Beat it, nerds!" Charlie said as she approached my trampoline with her crew—Mandy, Kelsey, and Laney. Charlie's friends were just as popular as Charlie was. They were all smart, funny, pretty, athletic, and were involved in just about every sport and club our school had to offer. All the girls wanted to be them, and all the guys wanted to date them. They were the "it crew," and my friends and I aspired to be just like them.

"Ummmm, no," I said in between bites of my pepperoni pizza. "Do I need to remind you that this is my trampoline Charlie, not yours?" I asked with a sly smirk on my face. My friends giggled, amused that for the first time I had something Charlie didn't have, and she wanted it.

Annoyed, Charlie quickly snatched the piece of pizza from my hand and mockingly said, "Do I need to remind you that I am older and stronger than you?" and then took a huge bite of my piece of pizza and smiled at her friends.

"Oh, snap!" Kelsey snickered at Charlie's insult.

"Whatever!" I sassed as I rolled my eyes at them. We had outgrown the days where Charlie would beat me up in order to get what she wanted. I knew she was just acting tough in front of her friends and that she wouldn't really hurt me. Little did Charlie know that I had a plan in mind that I had been saving for a hot day like today.

"Come on, girls," I said as I looked at my friends, "let's take our party inside." My friends didn't question me. They were used to the way Charlie treated me, and we were all used to the upperclassmen picking on us to get their way.

As my friends and I gathered up our pizza and drinks and hopped down off of the trampoline, Charlie and her friends snatched a few more pieces out of our box. But they couldn't bring us down; we were on natural high. We were ninth-graders!

"So what's the plan, Em?" Caroline asked as we set all the food and drinks down on the kitchen bar.

"Well, we're going to go to the pool anyway," I smiled, "so how about we get a little wet before we leave," I said as I grabbed a bag of water balloons out of the junk drawer in the kitchen and held it up for my friends to see.

We all laughed as we looked out the back window. Charlie and her friends were laughing and chanting "Seniors!" as they jumped on my trampoline. My friends and I smiled as we realized how clueless they were. They didn't know what was about to hit them— literally.

We split into groups to make the process go faster. Since there were two bathroom sinks and one kitchen sink, three of us filled the water balloons with cold water while the other three tied off the balloons and placed them into our empty backpacks. In no time we had a hundred balloons ready. Caroline, Sam, and Bailey each put on a backpack and headed out to the backyard. Lucy, Nina, and I followed closely behind. The bags were loaded and left partially unzipped allowing us easy access to our ammo. It was the perfect plan. Charlie and her crew couldn't see the water balloons in our backpacks; we were able to walk right up to the trampoline and unleash our freshman wrath on the senior tyrants. Operation Claim Our Trampoline was on!

Charlie, Laney, Kelsey, and Mandy all screamed as we pegged them one by one with the water balloons. My friends and I all laughed as we continued to hit my sister and her friends. They shrieked louder and louder as each cold water balloon exploded on their bodies. After the initial shock wore off, Charlie and her friends realized where the water balloons were coming from—our backpacks. They all jumped off the trampoline and began fighting us for the water balloons. My friends fought hard, but Mandy, Kelsey, and Laney were bigger and stronger. They were able to steal most of them from the bag and pop them over our heads and peg various parts of our bodies with them. Within minutes, all of us were wet and laughing as the battle of the seniors versus the freshman continued.

As the battle was coming to an end, Charlie ran to the side of the house and grabbed the water hose. She quickly unwound the hose, turned it on full blast, and aimed it at me and my friends. In the process of spraying us she accidentally soaked her friends as well. Annoyed, we looked at one another and gave an understanding head nod to join forces to attack Charlie. Laughter filled the air as we hit Charlie from all angles with the remaining water balloons while she fought us off with the water hose.

Within minutes everyone was dripping wet from head to toe. Surprisingly, instead of being annoyed with her little sister and her sister's annoying friends, Charlie and her crew were laughing just as hard as we were. Although they didn't admit it, they were having fun hanging with the loser freshmen a.k.a. "frosh."

"Props, frosh," Kelsey said as she patted me on the back a little too hard, and said, "You're annoying, but I like your style!" Kelsey and Charlie had been friends for years, and she had often stood up for me whenever Charlie was picking on me.

"Guess you freshman are smarter than you look!" Mandy teased.

"Well, she is my sister," Charlie said and put me in a headlock and gave me a quick noogie. She released me from her grip and said, "Alright nerds, I guess you guys can hang out with us for a little bit," and shrugged her shoulders and added, "You earned it."

My friends and I looked at one another in disbelief. Not only had Charlie and her cool friends just given us a compliment but also they were allowing us to stick around and "hang" with them. Although summer had only started a couple of hours ago, it was already shaping up to be one of the best ones yet!

My friends and I eagerly ran inside and grabbed the rest of the pizza, sodas, and chips while Charlie and her friends dragged the porch chairs and table to the sides of the trampoline. After all the snacks were set up, Charlie plugged in her CD player to the outside porch outlet. Within minutes the McCoy backyard was bumping! We had a mini party going on without even having planned one.

It was midday, and the sun was shining down on us. As we waited for our clothes and the trampoline to dry off, we ate, talked, and listened to music. Once everyone was dry we decided to keep the party going by dividing into two teams—a team of judges and a team of competitors—and have a jump-off. Since all of us were on the cheer squad, the competition was cutthroat. As the judges eliminated the contestants one by one, Charlie and I were the last two remaining. In the end, Charlie ended up beating me by a fraction of a decimal point causing all my friends to boo and holler "Cheaters!" at the seniors. As we joked that the seniors had cheated, they called us lame and threatened to stop playing our childish games. However, instead of getting up and leaving, Charlie and her friends continued on with our "childish games."

As the afternoon passed, we came up with game after game after game. Each passing game got a little sillier, a little more fun, and definitely more dangerous. At one point we were all taking turns jumping from the tire swing and onto the trampoline. Summer excitement filled the air as we continued to feed off of each other's energy—laughing, smiling, and getting crazier by the minute. Before we knew it, we were moving the trampoline from the middle of the backyard up to the back porch.

The McCoy back porch was a popular hangout because it was covered by an overhanging roof. When you grow up without a basement, you come to value a porch like ours. It offered a private place to hang that was outside of a parent's hearing range. It was also accessible from Charlie's bedroom window. As teenagers, Charlie and her friends liked to sleep over so they could sneak out through her window. It was only about a six-foot drop from the porch roof to the ground. Once on the roof, they'd lie on their stomachs and slowly lower themselves until they were hanging by their fingertips, and then they could make the remaining drop injury free.

That covered porch served as inspiration for the most dangerous trampoline challenge of the day. Someone—most likely Charlie—suggested climbing out the bedroom window and onto the porch roof then jumping off the roof and onto the trampoline. Sounds stupid, I know, but we were young, carefree, invincible (we thought), and did many, many stupid things. Jumping off the roof to the trampoline was probably one of the stupidest things I did during my childhood.

Charlie, being the biggest daredevil of us all, was the first to jump off the porch roof and onto the trampoline at least six feet below. We all stood in the yard below chanting "Jump! Jump! Jump!" as we watched in nervous envy as Charlie both bravely and stupidly jumped off the roof and onto the trampoline below. She jumped with so much force that when her feet met the trampoline, the middle of the trampoline almost touched the ground before sending Charlie soaring back into the air. Charlie's body projected diagonally through the air, and she somehow managed to land feet first on the ground five feet away from the trampoline. We all jumped up and down and screamed in excitement as Charlie faced us and gave us a bow.

"That was awesome!" Charlie screamed. Kelsey, Laney, and Mandy ran towards her and tackled her as if she was a football player who had just scored the winning touchdown with a few seconds remaining on the clock.

Once we saw how high Charlie soared through the air from off the trampoline and had landed safely on the ground unharmed, we all wanted to give it a try. Like I said, we were all cheerleaders, so we were used to jumping. To us, the higher the better! Once again we divided into groups of competitors and judges. While the judges sat in the yard below ready to witness the best jumps ever, the competitors climbed out of Charlie's window and stood on the roof anxiously awaiting their turn.

Everyone's first round of jumps was a little timid. We needed to test the waters to see how fast and far the initial drop from the roof to the trampoline was. Once we conquered the initial fear of jumping, we became more confident and more creative. Instead of just a straight jump off the roof, we would do toe touches and other cheer jumps. Some of us even braved a front flip from the roof to the trampoline.

In between turns, the group waiting to jump entertained the judges below by dancing to the music blaring from Charlie's CD. We were oblivious to the shingles falling off the porch roof, and no one heard the creaking of wood as eight grown teenage girls waited their turn to shine.

Since school had let out at noon, by the time the roof competition started we only had an hour or so before Mom was due home from work. Charlie and I both knew Mom wouldn't approve of the roof competition; however, we were having too much fun and weren't paying attention to the time. We were too caught up in the excitement of being young, carefree, and being on summer vacation to foresee what was about to happen.

Lucy and I had made it to the finals, and I was the last one to compete. I watched Lucy do a prefect toe touch off the roof then land on the trampoline. Once her feet hit the trampoline, she bounced back into the air to do yet another perfect toe touch, and finally she ended her routine with a front flip. With a routine like that, I knew she was in the lead, and I had to do something extreme to beat her.

As I planned my jumps, I stepped to the middle of the roof to warm up my legs and did several quick jumps in a row. Each time my feet landed on the porch roof, it seemed to shake a little bit beneath my feet. I thought I was just imagining things; however, as I walked from the middle to the edge of the roof, there was noticeable shaking and loud creaking—so loud that I could hear it over the music blaring below and my friends chanting my name. The shaking roof caused my knees to buckle, and I knew something terrible was about to happen.

I was overtaken by fear as I quickly jumped off the roof just as the middle of it caved in and came crashing down on the porch below. As I soared through the air, everything seemed to happen in slow motion. I could hear the loud banging of wood and shingles falling down onto the brick patio below. As I hit the trampoline, I turned my head to witness pieces of roof continuing to fall down and my friends running away from the patio to avoid getting hit by the debris. Then as I hit the trampoline, it flung me in an awkward direction, and I looked towards Charlie to see a combination of pure disbelief and horror plastered on her face as she watched and yelled, "Oh, [BLEEP]!" Finally all the banging and crashing noises stopped just as I came to an ungraceful landing on the ground. Upon hitting the ground, instant pain coursed through my right foot and ankle. I was fairly confident I had just sprained or broken something, but that was the least of my concerns.

I slowly and carefully stood up and turned to see how bad the damage was. As I turned, I saw all our friends standing frozen in their places, mouths hanging to the ground as they stared ahead. I didn't want to look, but I knew I had to. What had been an intact back roof only moments ago was now a huge messy pile of wood, shingles, and nails covering the entire brick patio. I gasped in disbelief.

This mistake was just as bad, if not worse than, the time Charlie and Liz shattered the back window. There was no cleaning this mess up before Mom got home, and there was no way to hide it from her. We could have picked up all the pieces and thrown them into the firewood pile, but it wouldn't take long for her to notice that almost the entire back porch roof was missing.

To make matters worse, we couldn't even get into the house to retrieve our friends' belongings so they could leave before Mom came home. We all just stood there in silence. The fallen broken roof pieces had broken Charlie's CD player, and just like the fallen pieces had crushed it, so were my summer plans. I knew that this mistake was it for Charlie and me. Summer had started four hours ago, and now summer was ending for us.

Charlie was the first to speak. "Okay, everyone, we need to act fast!" Fear filled her voice. "Help me move the trampoline back to its original place. There's a chainsaw in the barn. We need to cut down the tree limb and stage it to look like it fell on top of the roof," she commanded.

No one questioned her; we all sprang into action. As everyone else sprinted to the trampoline, I quickly limped my way over to it, and we all worked together to push it back to its original spot in the yard. Just as we were finished moving the trampoline, we all turned to witness the wrath of Mom.

"What the [BLEEP] is going on here?" Mom screamed as she stood in her high heels and dress clothes and looked at the horrid pile of rubbish. She threw her purse to the ground and quickly paced back and forth and side to side examining what had once been our back porch. As she surveyed the backyard, it didn't take her long to realize the brand-new trampoline had something to do with this mess.

"Charlotte Ann McCoy! Emily Kathleen McCoy!" Mom screamed. "Get over here! Now! The rest of you, leave!"

As our friends scattered, Charlie and I held our heads low as we slowly and fearfully walked over to Mom. Needless to say, Mom was beyond mad. Charlie and I found ourselves crying as Mom unleashed her wrath upon the both of us and took no pity.

Did we do something wrong? Absolutely. Were we reckless?

Most definitely. Did we mean to bring the porch roof down? Hell, no! Was Mom going to make us pay for it? You'd better believe it. And pay for it we did! What had started out as the "summer of Emily" and the "summer of Charlie" quickly turned into "kiss summer goodbye" for both Charlie and me. Mom took down the trampoline and took the pieces to Apple's house. As for paying for the damages, we once again found ourselves working for Mom and babysitting the bratty kids down the street just as Liz and Charlie had done when they had to pay for the back window.

As for Charlie and me, we did what we did best—blamed each other. However, those few hours when Charlie and her friends and me and my friends all laughed and hung out were priceless. For a brief moment, Charlie and I were friends instead of sisters. Looking back, I wish us McCoy Boys would have known what we know now—that life really does pass in the blink of an eye, and throughout your life friends will come and go, but you'll always have your family. Those moments when we all got along and acted like not only friends but sisters who loved and cared for one another were some of the best moments of my life.

McCoy for President

The summer of 1999 had ended, and the first day of my freshman year and Charlie's senior year arrived. We grabbed our book bags, gave Mom a quick kiss, and rushed out the door eager to get to school. Nervous energy filled Charlie's car as we pulled into the parking lot of Deer Park High School. Upon parking, Charlie took off her seatbelt, looked over at me, and said, "No offense, but this is my senior year, and I can't be seen walking in with a freshman."

"Really, Charlie?" I moaned and rolled my eyes at her and unbuckled my seatbelt, ready to get out of the car.

"I'm not asking for you to wait in the car all day; just give me a head start," she said as she opened the driver's side door.

"Whatever. Have a great first day," I said sarcastically to her as she jumped out of the car and ran to meet up with Laney and Kelsey, who were parked a few rows away.

My first day of high school was nerve-racking. The majority of my classes were honors classes, which meant I was in class with mostly tenth-graders. Luckily for me, Caroline, Lucy, and Nina were in honors classes as well. The tenth-graders were annoyed to have us freshmen intruding on their classes, but as long as we were together we didn't care. We sat next to one another in class and met up with Bailey and Sam in the hallway between classes and somehow managed to survive our first day of high school.

As I adjusted to juggling nightly soccer and cheer practice, along with spending hours a night on homework, the first couple of weeks of high school passed stressfully and slowly. Each day started out the same—me waiting in the car until Charlie was a safe distance ahead then meeting up with my friends. My friends and I would try to keep a low profile as we walked through the high school hallways and in class so as to not draw much attention to ourselves. We were still trying to figure out how to fit in. When Charlie and her friends would pass us in the hall, we'd all stare at them willing them to say hi to us; however, they'd continue on with their conversation and ignore us lowly freshmen.

At the end of the second week of school, things slowly began to change for my friends and me. While sitting in honors algebra at the last bell of the day, afternoon announcements came on: "Teachers, pardon the interruption," our principal Mr. Price's voice came from the speakers hanging above the clock, "The results of the student government elections are in. I'll begin with announcing the winners of the senior class. Congratulations to the new senior class secretary, Mandy Walker; the treasurer, Laney Geers; the new vice president, Kelsey Holland; and for the senior class president, congratulations to Miss Charlie McCoy!"

I rolled my eyes and let out a sigh—as if Charlie and her friends needed to win anything else. I listened as he went through the junior class, followed by the sophomore class. When he announced the sophomore vice president, half of my class applauded and gave high fives to a boy sitting three seats in front of me. I froze in my seat as Mr. Price announced the winners for ninth-grade student government.

"Congratulations to the ninth-grade secretary, Sam Montgomery; treasurer, Caroline Johnson; to the vice president, Nina Davidson; and finally, last but not least, for ninth-grade president, Miss Emily McCoy! Congratulations to the McCoys. I think this is the first time this school has ever had sisters holding class president positions."

My heart was pounding with excitement! Not only was I happy for my friends but I couldn't believe I had won class president! I looked over to Nina sitting next to me, and from the expression on her face I could tell she was just as shocked and happy as I was. It wasn't every day that you and your best friend are elected vice president and president by your classmates. Speechless, all we could do was grin from ear to ear.

My trance was broken by Anthony, a cute tenth-grader sitting in front of me, turning around and saying, "Congratulations, Emily and Nina!"

Immediately my cheeks turned red, flushed from embarrassment. I didn't even know a boy as cute as Anthony knew my name.

"Thanks, Anthony!" Nina and I both said at the same time. Then congratulations started to come from all around the room, and Nina and I continued to graciously smile and nod thank you to everyone.

"All right, everyone," Mrs. Roe said, "since there are only a few minutes left for the day, you may talk quietly among yourselves."

Just as I was turning to talk to Nina, I was surprised to see Anthony turn back around and say, "I didn't know you're Charlie's little sister."

"Yup, that's me, the youngest McCoy." My heart dropped with the realization that he was only interested in talking to me because I was Charlie's little sister.

"That's cool!" he said, "I'm the youngest Smith boy. I think my oldest brother Marcus graduated with your sister Liz," he said.

"Oh yeah, I remember Marcus," I smiled back and added, "He was a football player. He and Liz would hang out after the games."

"I play football too," Anthony beamed. "I think I saw you at cheer practice the other day while we were running a drill."

"Um, yeah," I stuttered, surprised that he noticed me. "I'm a cheerleader," I said nervously. At first I thought Anthony was talking to me just because Mr. Price had pointed out to the entire school that I was Charlie McCoy's sister, but now I realized that he had been watching me at cheer practice. And with that, the bell rang.

"Cool. Well, I'll see ya around at practice tonight then," Anthony said as he sprang out of his chair.

"Yup! See ya!" I said a little too eagerly as I remained sitting in my chair, still a little shocked that within five minutes I had won class president and had a cute older boy talk to me.

Nina and I squealed with excitement as we left the classroom. As we walked down the hall, people we didn't expect to know our names were congratulating us and giving us high fives. That's when I realized that one of the best things about being in a small school is that everyone knows everything about everyone. Throughout my high school years, this would be both a curse—like when I'd do something embarrassing or wrong—and a blessing—like in my current moment of winning class president.

That day, as my group of friends walked out the doors, we passed Charlie and her friends standing outside the gym. Instead of ignoring us like they had done many times before, they did something I didn't see coming—they acknowledged our existence!

"Look out DP, the McCoy sisters are taking over!" Kelsey yelled over to me and then laughed.

Excitedly, my friends and I slowed our pace, and I replied, "You know it! Congratulations, Kelsey, Laney, and Mandy!"

"Excuse me; you forgot someone!" Charlie piped in from the middle of her group.

"Oh, did I?" I teased.

"You can always walk home!" Charlie threatened as her friends chuckled.

From that day on, whenever Charlie's group of friends would pass my group of friends in the hallway, they continued to acknowledge us. At first it was just a head nod or a smile, but then the head nods slowly turned into high fives or a "Whaz up, frosh."

Yes, they ignored us at Homecoming, but Charlie did surprise me by letting Mom take pictures of us together before we left in separate cars to go to the dance. By the time Christmas break rolled around, Charlie and I were gossiping on the car rides to school while we sang along to music just as Liz and Charlie had done. And thanks to the cold and snowy Cincinnati weather, she stopped making me wait in the car to give her a head start before I was allowed to get out of the car. Instead, we started to have mini snowball fights to see who could hit the other one first. Charlie had better aim than I did and won every time. However, what Charlie didn't realize was that while we were having our friendly snowball competition, she was walking into school with a nerdy freshman— but I believe that secretly she didn't mind.

"It's the End of the World as We Know It"

It was Christmas Day. After unwrapping presents at Mom's, we jumped in the car and drove four streets away to Dad's. We were stunned as we entered his house. Yes, Dad always had Christmas decorations—a Christmas tree along with stockings hung by the chimney with care—but his house was normally decorated like a bachelor pad. Until this Christmas morning we had never seen a Christmas wonderland quite like this before.

In the living room Jimmy Buffet Christmas music was playing. A ceramic Christmas village was lit up on the mantle, with overflowing stockings hanging below. A Christmas brunch fit to feed the entire street awaited us on the dining room table. What really caught our eye were the large stacks of presents underneath the Christmas tree. Growing up in middle-class Ohio, my parents had always saved throughout the year to splurge on Christmas presents, but nothing like this. The stacks of presents wouldn't even fit under the tree. They took up half the living room. We all stood in the doorway speechless staring at the presents.

Liz was the first to break the silence. "What the—"

"Ho! Ho! Ho!" Liz was interrupted by Santa Dad pouncing into the living room. If our jaws weren't hanging to the floor before, they were now. In front of us stood Dad in a full-blown Santa suit—beard, hat, black boots, and all. This was something he had never done for us, not even as young girls.

"Merry Christmas, girls!" Santa Dad exclaimed as he approached us, embracing us in long, emotional hugs.

"Um, Dad," Charlie began as she broke away from Dad's lingering hug, "what's going on here?" she asked as she motioned to all the presents.

"What do you mean?" Santa Dad asked befuddled.

"What she means is what's up with all these [bleeping] presents?" Liz didn't waste time getting straight to the point.

"It's Christmas!" Dad exclaimed. "It only comes once a year," he said as he added a "Ho! Ho! Ho!" and rubbed his belly. "So come in, and let's get started!" he said excitedly.

Hesitantly we all took off our snowy boots and jackets and made our way to the couch.

Santa Dad eagerly grabbed our stockings from the mantle and gave one to each of us.

Candy, lottery tickets, flashlights, and goodies just kept coming. Lastly, all of our stockings contained a white envelope.

"You have to open those at the same time," Santa Dad instructed.

We all looked at one another and nodded, giving the go to open the envelopes. Inside were Christmas cards with a heartfelt message from Dad telling us how much he loved us, along with a wad of cash and instructions to buy something nice for ourselves.

My eyes grew wide as I began to count the pile of cash—twenty, eighty, one hundred, one hundred twenty, one-eighty, two hundred?! I hadn't held this much cash in my hands in my entire life! I sat there staring at the money calculating how many hours I'd have to babysit the bratty little kids down the street to earn two hundred dollars and contemplating what I was going to buy with all this dough. And then I realized that Dad wouldn't give me two hundred dollars without giving Liz and Charlie the same amount. This meant Dad had just given us a total of six hundred dollars! My stomach tightened with fear; something was gravely wrong with Dad. I swallowed hard and looked at my sisters. They were both holding their wad of twenties in their hands looking at each other with the same concerned-filled eyes.

"All right," Charlie was the first to break the awkward silence, "who's dying?" she asked as she threw her wad of cash onto the coffee table in front of us.

"I'm with Charlie!" I squeaked, following suit and throwing my money down next to hers. If there was something wrong with Dad, I wanted nothing to do with that money.

"What the [BLEEP] is going on?" Liz threw her money on top of ours, stood up, and began frantically pacing the living room.

Santa Dad sat in the recliner looking at us with a shocked expression on his face. "Nothing!" he defended himself. "I just wanted to give you girls the Christmas you've always deserved," he reasoned.

"I don't buy it!" Charlie exclaimed. "Liz is in college, Em and I are in high school, and you just gave each of us two hundred bucks…in cash," she exclaimed, "not to mention, we still have a mound of presents to unwrap! Something is wrong," she said nervously.

I nodded in agreement as my stomach tightened even harder. Not knowing what was wrong with Dad was making me feel sick.

"We are not unwrapping any of these presents until you tell us the truth," Liz protested. "Do you have cancer? How much time did they give you?" Tears filled her eyes.

Dad tore off his Santa hat and beard and threw them down on the floor. "Jesus! Can't I do something nice for my three girls without getting the third degree?!" He was obviously annoyed.

I felt bad for squelching Dad's Christmas spirit; however, I couldn't help but agree with my sisters. Dad had never given us so much money before; something was definitely wrong. We all just stared at Dad in disbelief waiting for him to tell us the truth.

"Dammit, girls, nothing is wrong, and I am not dying!" he said, looking defeated. "It's Christmas, and it's the first year I've had the money to spoil my girls like they deserve to be spoiled!" He ran his fingers through his curls. "So can't you girls just accept that nothing is wrong and unwrap your Christmas presents already! Please?!" Dad begged us.

We all looked at one another and nodded in agreement. Clearly Dad was in denial. We silently agreed that whatever Dad was going through he wasn't ready to tell us about. He was upset. None of us wanted to upset him on Christmas, so we all just needed to play along. We were old enough to realize that we needed to keep our mouths shut, put on a fake happy face, and unwrap our presents. Later we'd have a chance to investigate.

Liz walked over to the enormous stack of presents and grabbed one with my name on it. "This year, youngest goes first," she said as she handed me the present and gave me an understanding nod.

We spent the next hour taking turns unwrapping our presents, listening to Jimmy Buffet, and pretending we weren't worried about Dad. After brunch, my sisters and I gathered in the living room to examine all our gifts. We had received luggage sets, real gold jewelry, TVs, DVD players, clothes, and much, much more.

"Obviously something is wrong with Dad," Liz said. (Dad was in the bathroom getting cleaned up. The Santa suit had been warmer than he anticipated.) We all nodded our heads in agreement.

"And he's not going to tell us what it is," Charlie confirmed what we were all thinking.

"It's time to snoop!" I exclaimed.

We decided to split up to do a quick search through Dad's house before he was out of the shower. We needed to find something—anything—to give us a clue as to what was going on with Dad. Liz took his bedroom; Charlie, his living room; and I took the basement.

I opened the basement door and tried to quietly walk down the creaky old wooden stairs without making too much noise. I knew Dad was in the shower, but the bathroom was directly across from the basement door, and I didn't want him to know what we were up to. I entered the basement expecting to find the usual things he stored away for the winter—the outside porch furniture, his fishing gear and life vests, etc. At the end of the steps I turned on the basement lights, looked around, and stood speechless.

"What the—" I said out loud.

I tried to understand what I was seeing. To the left of the basement where there used to be a bare white wall now stood a shelving unit that I hadn't seen before. Not only did it cover the entire wall but it was filled completely with canned goods, bottled water, flashlights, batteries, drinks, toilet paper, paper towels, garbage bags, disinfectant wipes, and so much more. In the middle of the basement where Dad normally stored the back porch furniture now sat a twin bed with a comforter, pillow, and all. And finally, to the right of the basement, taking the place of Dad's fishing gear, hung several large guns. Sitting beneath the guns were a couch, table, radio, and lantern.

I stood there for several minutes turning my head from left to right, then right to left, trying to make sense of everything, but there was only one logical explanation—Dad had gone insane! Crazy thoughts began to race through my mind. Maybe he was hiding illegal immigrants in his basement. Or maybe one of my uncles had gotten into trouble with the law and was hiding out here. Or worse yet, maybe Dad had gotten into trouble with the law. I began to panic.

"Liz! Charlie!" I screamed, not caring if Dad heard me or not, "You guys gotta see this!" I called upstairs.

Liz and Charlie came running down the basement steps, where I stood frozen in my place, still taking it all in.

"What the [BLEEP] is going on down here?!" Liz exclaimed.

Charlie was the first to move and walk around the basement and garage while Liz and I stood befuddled. As she walked around she would randomly call out the weird stuff she'd find: "A ton of gasoline; not one but two refrigerators…" She paused as she opened them. "Correction: two freezers full of food!"

We had no idea what was going on. We must have lost track of time and forgotten to close the basement door because before we knew it, Dad was calling down to us.

"What are you girls doing down there?" Dad sounded angry.

We didn't want him to know we had discovered his weird secret, but it was too late. He ran down the basement steps to find us all wide-eyed and confused.

We all just looked at one another; none of us knew what to say.

Liz didn't bother trying to lie. "We were worried about you and wanted some answers. Want to tell us what all this crap is doing down here?" Liz motioned to the bed and everything else in the basement.

"Are you in some kind of trouble that we need to know about?" Charlie got straight to the point.

Dad's face was bright red. I couldn't tell if he was embarrassed or mad or both. He sat down on the couch.

"It's Y2K," he said as he shrugged.

I was confused. I knew that in a week we'd be starting a new millennium, but I wasn't sure what that had to do with all the crap in his basement.

"This" he said, extending his arms to the room, "is my bunker!"

"Your what?" I asked.

"My bunker," Dad repeated himself.

We all stood silently for a moment taking it all in. Charlie was the first to burst out laughing. Liz and I quickly joined in.

In a most serious tone Dad continued to defend himself. "What?" he asked as we continued to laugh. "You never know what can happen with Y2K! You have to be prepared, girls!"

Relief came over me as I laughed. I realized that no, my Dad was not dying, but yes, he was a little crazy. However, I'd take crazy over dying any day!

"I can't believe you, Dad!" Liz jokingly scorned.

"The world isn't going to end on January 1, 2000!" Charlie rubbed tears out of her eyes from making fun of our crazy dad.

"Well, if anything happens, at least you girls have a safe bunker to go to," Dad protested. "Taking care of you three girls is my job."

Now that we knew nothing was wrong with Dad other than his being a Y2K prepper, we spent the rest of Christmas Day laughing with Dad as we sorted through all our amazing gifts and ate our delicious feast.

When New Year's Eve came, my sisters and I couldn't help but call and torment Dad throughout the day warning him that there were only several hours left before the world would come to an end and to take cover in his bunker. We even went as far as to call and blare R.E.M.'s "It's the End of the World as We Know It" over the phone.

To this day I will never forget the uneasy feeling of watching the ball drop with my friends that New Year's Eve. As everyone around me happily smiled and screamed the final ten-second countdown, I remember anxiously holding my breath and closing my eyes. If Dad was right, and the world was going to end, I didn't want to see it going down. Once the room erupted with loud, excited "Happy New Year!" chants, I knew we had safely made it to midnight. I let out an audible sigh of relief and opened my eyes to see all the faces of my loving friends. I grabbed my phone, sent my sisters a quick "still alive" text, and then called Dad. He didn't answer his phone. (I guess he had forgotten to install a phone in his bunker!)

"The Times They Are a-Changin"

My freshman year and Charlie's senior year passed in the blink of an eye. After returning from Christmas break, Charlie continued to allow me to get out of the car at the same time as her, and in the hallways she continued to acknowledge my presence. No, we never attended the same parties, but at home she started giving me advice on my outfits and asking me real questions about my friends instead of just making fun of them. Sure, she'd pick on me from time to time and always have a good embarrassing story to share about me; however, things were beginning to feel different between us.

In the spring, Charlie ended up winning prom queen, and two weeks later she graduated at the top of her class. By August, she went off to Denison University, a college more than two hours away, on an academic scholarship, and I started my sophomore year of high school. On car rides to school, I went back to listening to Mom's oldies while she drove me, and my thoughts would drift off to my sisters—back to when I would listen to Liz and Charlie argue, laugh, and gossip, and then to the days when Charlie and I began to follow suit.

I continued to focus on playing soccer year-round and making good grades. Between sports, school, and hanging out with friends, I was able to keep myself occupied; however, neither school nor home was the same without Charlie around. The school halls weren't as interesting without Charlie and her crew walking around like they owned the place. After school, I'd come home to a quiet house where I was reminded that neither Liz nor Charlie would be coming home for dinner. The realization that both Liz and Charlie didn't live in our Glenbury home anymore began to hit me hard. After a couple of weeks, the void that filled our quiet house quickly filled my heart. Although my sisters could be ruthless at times, I had grown accustomed to a loud, chaotic home. When Liz went off to college, she was only a quick twenty-minute car ride away and came home often—not to mention, when Liz moved out, at least I still had Charlie at home pestering me.

Charlie's graduating and leaving for college was different than when Liz left. If I thought the house was quiet when Liz left, now the house was deafeningly silent. Also, unlike Liz, Charlie was a two-hour car ride away instead of a quick twenty minutes. To make matters worse, when Charlie left for college, she decided not to come home until Thanksgiving break. She thought this would be the easiest way for her to adjust to her new life, but I don't think she realized how hard it would be on the rest of the family. So at the start of the school year I was left with no sisters in the house to invade my privacy or to pry into my personal life; no one to ride to school with; no one to come home and talk to about all the latest Deer Park drama; no one to ask for advice; and no one to complain about Mom to. Now whose clothes could I steal when I needed something new to wear? And who was I going to take out my anger on when I'd had a bad day? Certainly not Mom! For the first time in my life, I knew what it felt like to be alone, and I didn't like it.

If I thought my sisters' leaving was hard on me, all I had to do was take one look at Mom to realize that I was getting off easy. For the first week after Liz and Charlie left, Mom looked like a sad, lost puppy looking for its owner. I could tell she wasn't ready for two of her three daughters to be out of the house and starting their young adult life—especially since in three short years her third and youngest child would follow closely in their footsteps leaving her completely alone.

Every night when she came home from work, she'd wander around aimlessly, disappointed at not seeing Charlie sitting at the bar eating a snack or Liz sitting on the couch reading. Now when she walked downstairs I was the only one sitting at the bar working on homework greeting her with a "Hey, Mom!" Even the things Liz and Charlie would do that annoyed her, she missed. She missed walking through the front door only to trip over Charlie's cheer bag that she always left out. She missed telling Liz to paint her nails at the table, not on the couch. When Mom went upstairs to change out of her work clothes, she'd sniff the air only to let out a sad sigh. Our upstairs no longer smelled like a combination of Charlie's hairspray and Liz's nail polish remover and perfume. The upstairs now smelled like my dirty soccer bag, but Mom was too sad to remind me to leave it downstairs in the laundry room. Although I was only a teenager, I knew my sisters' absence was harder on Mom than it was on me. In Mom's eyes, the Glenbury house that was once too crowded, too loud, and too messy with her three girls constantly fighting over our one shower was now feeling too big, too quiet, and too clean.

Although Dad's eyes weren't puffy and red like Mom's, he showed his sadness in different ways. Dad, who never came by the house uninvited, began regularly stopping by on his way home from work just to check in on Mom and me. Suddenly Dad's work day began to seem too long, and he started doing something he hadn't done before—leaving work early to be at all my home games. Yes, Dad came to sporting events, but due to work, he was normally there by halftime. Now he felt the urgency of time. In three years there wouldn't be any more home soccer, softball, or cheer games to come to. He kept a copy of my schedule front and center on his refrigerator, and any away game he couldn't make it to, he made sure to call me to hear how I played. Although I loved having my parents at all my events to cheer me on, I was beginning to worry that both Mom and Dad were on the verge of a mid-life crisis, and I was the only one left living at home to realize it or to do anything about it. Was I concerned about them? Yes, very much so. I love my parents. However, call me crazy, but keeping tabs on both parents' mental health was not my idea of fun and not the way I wanted to spend my last three years of high school!

Luckily for me, I wasn't as alone as I thought I was. One night when Liz wanted a home-cooked meal and clean clothes, she came home unannounced. To Liz's surprise, as she walked through the doors, she walked into an eerily quiet house with a sad, puffy-eyed mom eating dinner quietly alone. When she came up to my room, I eagerly stopped doing my homework and jumped up from my desk to hug her. Liz immediately expressed concern for Mom. I agreed and told her about Dad's new behavior. Before she left that night, she made a pact with me that she'd come home as often as she could and would help get our "old" parents back. Liz followed through with her end of the deal and for the following month came home every Wednesday night to eat dinner and watch TV with Mom and me. Afterwards she'd stop by Dad's to check in with him before going back to her sorority house. During those Wednesdays night dinners, Liz mostly talked to me about high school life and tried to bring Mom into the conversation by reminiscing on funny stories from her high school days. Mom would smile and laugh a little, but it was obvious that she was wishing the dining room table was complete with all three of her girls. After dinner, we all sat in awkward silence watching TV like zombies. When Liz and I would try to talk with Mom, she'd give a short response and stare off into space. It was clear that Mom's mind was someplace else. When Liz would get up to leave, Mom would give her a longer than usual hug and remind her about Sunday night family dinner.

From the time Charlie left until she came home for Thanksgiving break, Liz never missed a Sunday night family dinner. On Sundays Mom was always in a good mood because after family dinner came the highlight of her week—our weekly call to Charlie! During dinner, Mom, Liz and I would try to laugh and talk about silly things from the week; however, every dinner was the same. We'd all take a couple of bites of food, make small talk while we pushed the rest of the food around on our plates, and anxiously wait for the doorbell to ring. Mom would say, "Your dad's here! Time to call Charlie!"

I'd eagerly run upstairs to let Dad in while Mom would hit speed-dial on the phone, and Liz would stand next to her waiting for Charlie to answer. As soon as Charlie answered, Liz would hit the speaker button, and we'd all yell, "Hi Charlie!" then leave her on speaker while she filled us in on her week. After she finished giving us her weekly rundown, we'd take her off speaker and each take our five-minute turn to talk to her alone. Our privacy was limited to as far as the phone cord would stretch, which wasn't far, so the family member talking to her would walk between the laundry room and family room while everyone else sat in the family room and kitchen eavesdropping on one another's conversations.

Although Charlie missed us, she was doing well, and college life suited her. She had no problem making friends or adjusting to the coursework. Every Sunday for the thirty minutes we were gathered as a family talking on the phone with Charlie, life felt complete. During those conversations, my sisters resorted to nitpicking away on my personal life and calling me names. Instead of getting annoyed, I'd just roll my eyes and puff, "Whatever!" then continue filling them in on the high school drama from the week. My sisters and I would laugh, and Mom and Dad would smile. During those conversations, everyone was happy.

Then before we knew it, the thirty minutes would come to an end, and we were all forced to say our goodbyes. After we hung up the phone, Dad would give Liz and me a hug goodbye, and he'd leave. Mom would sit on the couch with a tissue dabbing tears from her eyes, and I would sit next to her lovingly patting her back. Liz would grab a pint of ice cream out of the freezer and three spoons and join Mom and me on the couch. We'd all sit in silence for a few minutes as we passed the pint of chocolate ice cream to one another taking one spoonful at a time. After a few minutes of silence, Liz would finally say, "Well, it sounds like Charlie is doing good!" and we'd all nod our heads in agreement. "Say Mom, did you hear…." and every week Liz had some new town gossip to distract Mom with—whether it was true or not; I never asked. All I know is that while Liz filled Mom in on the juicy gossip, Mom would sit there listening to the story, eyes wide, while she ate her ice cream. Even for just a few short minutes, her thoughts were diverted from thinking about how badly she missed Charlie and how badly she wanted all of us together again.

Looking back, Liz spent most of her childhood looking out for me, and then once Charlie left, she looked out for the entire family. When we needed it most, Liz was always good at making the family feel better. (Now I wonder who was there for Liz during those times.)

As the weeks slowly passed, the family began to adjust to being apart. During the week, instead of eating in sad silence, Mom and I started talking more to each other at the dinner table. I opened up to Mom about Homecoming and the girl drama over who was taking whom to the dance, and in return she filled me in on the drama at her work. And in the weeks to follow, instead of staring at the TV like zombies, we began to laugh out loud at our favorite TV shows. We were beginning to act like normal human beings again.

The days began to pass less painfully, and finally Thanksgiving arrived. For the first time since August, both Charlie and Liz came home, and once again the house was loud and crowded; Mom was beyond happy! For that week, we picked on one another just as we used to, got in silly arguments over nothing important, made fun of one another, laughed, cried, and annoyed Mom. It was amazing! Most nights we'd stay up late watching our favorite movies or playing board games while we talked and ate entirely too much junk food. On those nights, my sisters and I deemed ourselves too tired to move, so we would just camp out in the living room instead of going upstairs to bed. And it was during the wee hours of the morning that we would start talking and laughing as friends do instead of sisters who had lived in a constant state of war with one another.

Charlie's leaving for college had changed everything between us. Somehow we were more tolerant of each other. We began to really listen as the other talked, and my sisters started giving me actual advice instead of just making fun of my life. Yes, we still picked on one another, but it was different. Our jokes weren't out of anger or intended to hurt one another; instead they were intended to make one another laugh about the things happening in our lives that were hard and that we had no control over.

We spent Thanksgiving at Dad's, and for the first time all helped Dad cook. We laughed as Liz messed up every side dish she touched, and we put her in charge of the rolls. To this day Charlie and I are the cooks, and we often leave Liz in charge of something simple. After dinner we returned home to Mom's to continue with family games and dessert. That week the family was happy, complete. But like all good times do, Thanksgiving break passed much too quickly and came to a heart-wrenching end. At the end of the week, it was time for Charlie to make the two-hour car ride back to Denison and for Liz to return to her sorority house.

That night as my sisters drove away, Mom and I both clung to each other and cried. As Mom hugged me, she told me not to worry, that in a few short weeks both Liz and Charlie would be home for Christmas break, and then after that, they'd be home for spring break, and then finally they'd be back for the entire summer! However, when she released me from her grip and I looked into her eyes, I wasn't sure if she was trying to reassure herself or me. Whatever the case, her words held truth, and from that day on, we both tried to live day to day on the promise that it wouldn't be long until the entire family was all together. Somehow Mom's words made us realize that the quiet and lonely house was only temporary and that in a few short months the house would return to our normal hectic McCoy Boys Home, and this made the days easier.

Liz continued to come home for Sunday night dinners but stopped checking in on Mom and Dad during the week. By Easter, Mom and I had adjusted to our new home life—a life where Charlie and Liz were only a phone call away; a life that wasn't as eventful as it once had been when all three of us crazy hormonal teenage girls lived together under the same roof but still was good; a life where the distance between us made us all—even Charlie—appreciate our crazy family even more. For the McCoy Boys, the saying, "Absence makes the heart grow fonder," definitely held true.

"All the Single Ladies"

My high school years passed much too quickly. Between my friends, sports, academics, and work, I hardly had any free time. Although Mom and I adjusted to living in a less chaotic home, I still missed having my sisters around and looked forward to family dinners, phone calls, and my sisters coming home for holiday breaks. Throughout my junior and senior years, Liz and Charlie made a point to come home for all my important events such as dances, parades, and my soccer senior night. Just as Liz had been Charlie's personal hair and makeup artist for Homecoming, she was mine too. During the parade my sisters held up a sign saying "Emmie the Hemi for Queen" and I laughed and waved at them as I sat perched on the back of Aunt Anne's convertible just as Charlie had done. Although I didn't win homecoming queen, I was happy to see my sisters cheering me on in the crowd and happy to see my best friend, Nina, wear the crown.

During these years, my sisters and I connected with one another the best way we knew how—by making all our achievements a friendly sisterly competition. When I started to hang with some older kids that were more party animals than bookworms, Charlie taunted me with "You know, my high school GPA was higher than yours." Naturally this gave me the push I needed to get my grades back on track. I loved to write but never thought anything could come from my hobby. Liz encouraged me to join our school's writing team as she had done with "I was runner-up in our writing competition; think you could beat me?" Although I never won any awards, Liz would come home to proofread my writing, and her encouragement and interest was reward enough. Without realizing it, everything I did during my high school years became a friendly competition among my sisters and me. And when I had something to celebrate, it always made our phone calls more interesting.

I remember boasting through the phone, "Charlie! Guess who made captain of the soccer team… as a junior!"

"No way, Em! That's awesome! I was never captain as a junior!" Charlie gushed in envy.

"Well, I just did!" I sang as Charlie laughed.

And just as they were there to celebrate my accomplishments with me, they were also there for me when I needed comfort.

"Man, Liz, my writing didn't get picked…again," I pouted over the phone to Liz.

"What? I can't believe that! I loved that piece," Liz comforted me.

"Me, too," I sulked.

"Don't let it get you down, Em. You can't win them all. There's always next year!" she encouraged me.

Not only were my sisters and I learning to have fun while living apart but Mom and I began to have a little more fun as well. Now that I was "an only child," our house quickly became our go-to hangout for my friends and me—fire pits, Halloweens parties, you name it. Mom was grateful to be the host and to have the Glenbury house lively again.

I was bonding more not only with my friends but with my family as well. We would play dominoes at Apple's house on Sundays after church. In the fall, Dad and I would bond over cheering on our football team, the Cincinnati Bengals, on TV while we grilled out. I had never had one-on-one time like this with my parents before, and although I was a teen who was often too cool for my parents, I secretly really enjoyed their undivided attention.

One Saturday night after cheering for our varsity basketball team in a tournament, Caroline, Bailey, Lucy, Nina, Sam, and I headed to our local T.G.I. Friday's to eat. Upon walking in, the restaurant bar area was decorated with huge signs indicating that our local radio station was there live on air. Hanging above the bar was a sign that read "Help Dennis Find a Date." My friends and I took an immediate interest. Who was Dennis, and why was the local radio station here? As the waitress showed us to our table, she filled us in on all the details.

Dennis was a local looking for a date for Valentine's Day. The radio station was running a segment every day in February leading up to Valentine's Day. Each day they featured a different local man or woman searching for love. The radio station had asked their listeners to call if you were interested in participating. That night they were encouraging female listeners who might be looking for love to come out and meet Dennis.

My friends and I all looked at one another. We could see the wheels turning in one another's minds. Dennis looked to be around all our parents' age, and for a middle-aged man he was decent-looking.

"Give them your mom's number!" Caroline was the first to say what we were all thinking.

"Yes! Hook a mother up!" Bailey laughed.

"Ha!" I chuckled. "She'd kill me! But…I like the way you girls think!" I flashed my friends a mischievous smile.

Before our waitress was back with our drinks, I was over at the bar talking to the radio crew.

Within minutes, my Mom and I were live on air! T.G.I. Friday's had the conversation playing through its sound system.

"Hey, Mom!" I said as she answered the phone.

"Hey, Em. If you're calling to see if you can stay out later, the answer is no; we have church in the morning."

"And what church do you go to?" Kevin, the radio host, interrupted.

"Emily?" Mom asked.

"This is Kevin from 92.1 Deer Park Live. I'm here at T.G.I. Friday's with your lovely daughter Emily, and we are live on air," Kevin said enthusiastically.

"The radio station?" Mom asked surprised. "Did we win something?" Excitement filled her voice.

"Well, if you come on up to T.G.I. Friday's, you might win something." Kevin answered.

"What can I win?" Mom inquired.

"Your daughter tells us you're single." Kevin waited for confirmation from Mom.

"Um... yes," Mom said, unsure of how being single had anything to do with winning a prize.

"Well, after tonight, you might not be single anymore! We have Dennis here looking for love."

"Oh, goodness!" Mom said. "Um, thank you for the offer, but I think I'll pass," Mom politely declined.

"Well, tonight we're not taking no for an answer. We already sent our limo to your house to pick you up. We'll see you soon," Kevin said as he hung up the phone, not giving Mom a chance to say no again.

Within seconds of walking away from the bar and back to the table where my friends all sat laughing and cheering, my cell phone rang. It was Mom.

"You're grounded!" was all she said before she hung up the phone.

"Uh-oh, Em," Lucy laughed at me when I sat down next to her. She could hear Mom yelling through the phone.

I shrugged my shoulders. I knew I was in trouble, but—who knew?—maybe Mom would end up liking this Dennis guy. Since my parents divorced, neither of them had ever gone out on a date. My sisters and I grew up in a very unique divorced family. My parents were always kind to each other, and we all gathered for holidays and celebrations. Dad and Mom always helped each other out. If Mom needed something fixed in the house, Dad would come over to fix it. If Dad needed help buying birthday or Christmas presents, Mom would do his shopping. My sisters and I are eternally grateful that our parents put aside their differences and always did what was best for their girls; however, now that I was almost grown, I couldn't help but think that maybe it was time for the two of them to put themselves out there and date.

As our food arrived, my friends and I could see the limo pull up in front of the restaurant. Several women got out of the back, including Mom. Before going to the bar to meet Dennis, Mom found our table and approached us. "You and I are having a nice long talk when we get home, young lady," Mom said in a stern voice before putting on a fake smile and walking away.

"Oh man, Em," Nina said, "you may have gone too far this time!"

"Nah," I said, although I was secretly frightened that Nina was right. "I'm almost out of the house; it's time for her to date," I said.

"Carpe diem!" Sam said, and we all raised our sodas and "cheered" one another.

My friends and I watched as my mom awkwardly sat next to Dennis at the bar and talked as she drank a beer. We played a game trying to figure out what they were talking about and what Dennis' life story was. My friends and I decided Dennis was an accountant. He had been married before, but sadly his wife had left him for an Italian man and moved to Italy leaving him alone to raise his good-looking son, who was our age, all by himself. Not only was he smart and funny but he had an amazing beach house in Florida that he ever so graciously invited Mom and me (and all my friends, of course) to come visit over Spring Break. Naturally, we all accepted his invitation, and my friends were happy to see that his son had invited all his good-looking friends too.

However, none of our assumptions were true, and Mom and Dennis didn't fall in love. Mom stayed for a couple of drinks and an appetizer, but by the time we were all finished eating and had paid our bill, Mom was ready to go. Mom hitched a ride home with us in Lucy's mom's van. At first Mom was quiet; however, as we all told Mom our made-up scenario about Dennis, she couldn't help but chuckle.

At the end of the night, Mom forgave me. Although she didn't find love that night, she did get free drinks and an appetizer, got to ride in a limo, was live on the radio, and lived to tell a pretty interesting story. To this day, Mom and Dad have never dated anyone.

Secrets

Before I knew it, Thanksgiving of my senior year of high school arrived. We were all gathered at Mom's for Thanksgiving when Charlie threw our family a major curve ball. She was excited to announce that after Christmas she'd be studying abroad in Australia. I think Mom almost choked on her turkey as she scorned her with "What? You didn't ask your mother for permission, young lady!" and Liz jealously threw down her fork and protested, "So unfair! I'm the oldest, and I should be the first to travel some place cool." While Dad sat wide-eyed and shocked, unsure of what to say, he stressfully rubbed his forehead and remained silent.

Charlie just politely shrugged her shoulders and replied, "You don't need to worry about me, Mom. I'm an adult now, and besides, it's a once-in-a-lifetime opportunity! Not to mention, my application has already been approved," she smiled as she reached across the table to hold Mom's shaking hand. Then Charlie turned to Liz and said, "I'll take plenty of pictures for you, Liz," and smiled as she stuck her tongue out.

"Gee, thanks." Liz rolled her eyes and laughed.

Was I surprised? No. Charlie has always been the adventurous one. Were my parents surprised? More like shocked and completely devastated! Their middle daughter was going to not only travel outside of the country for the first time but travel to the opposite side of the globe! I mean, they don't call it "the land down under" for nothing. In my parents' eyes, Charlie might just as well have been traveling to Mars!

Before Charlie left for her three-month journey, Mom gave her three specific rules to follow: no body piercings or tattoos; no skydiving; and lastly—the most important rule of all—no falling in love with an Australian! *Really, Mom? Haven't you learned by now that it's in every child's, teenager's, and young adult's DNA to find a way to do exactly what their parents tell them NOT to do?*

Three months later when Charlie returned, Dad, Mom, Liz, and I all gathered at the airport. We stood in front of the windows overlooking the terminal and held up several embarrassing signs as we anxiously awaited Charlie's arrival.

Charlie eagerly ran towards us screaming our names in excitement. We threw down our signs and just as eagerly screamed "Charlie!" and ran towards her. As both Mom and Dad clung to their middle child, I couldn't help but notice tears of relief streaming from their eyes.

At first glance, I almost didn't recognize Charlie. Not only was she golden tan with blonde highlights streaked throughout her dark brown hair but when she spoke, she now had a slight Australian accent. However, one of the more noticeable changes in Charlie's appearance was a small diamond stud nose ring sparkling from her left nostril. I waited for Mom to say something— anything—but she continued to cling to Charlie and cry, "We're so glad you're home!"

"Okay, Mom," Liz interrupted, "if you squeeze her too tightly she just might pop!"

I laughed as Mom finally released her grip on Charlie and said, "Tell us ALL about your trip!"

As Dad retrieved Charlie's luggage from baggage claim, Charlie couldn't get the pictures from her trip out of her purse fast enough. While we waited on Dad, she showed Liz, Mom, and me her pictures. The first photo she showed us was one of…wait for it…wait for it…Charlie skydiving! Wide-eyed, I glanced at the photo and then at Mom. I put one arm around Mom's lower back waiting for her to drop over dead from shock, but to my surprise, all Mom did was shake her head in utter disapproval. That's when I realized that between the nose ring and the skydiving, Charlie could tell Mom anything, and Mom wasn't going to lecture her. Right now, all Mom and Dad cared about was that Charlie was home safe and sound.

Charlie noticed the disapproving scowl on Mom's face and tried to reassure her. "I survived, Mom! And it was amazing!" Charlie continued to beam as she gave Mom a quick kiss on the cheek.

Mom remained silent, and Liz encouraged Charlie to show us more pictures. Charlie showed us breathtaking sunsets, crystal clear blue water, exotic animals like kangaroos and koalas, pictures of her scuba diving, and then pictures of the her at the beach with a good-looking, curly-haired, green-eyed guy.

"Hold the phone! Who's that hottie?" Liz asked wide-eyed.

"Campbell," Charlie practically sung his name.

Although I was only eighteen, I couldn't help but notice the I'm-in-love glow painted all over Charlie's face. I gawked at my sister in envy; she was the happiest I had ever seen her. She had just traveled out of the country and somehow managed to break all of Mom's rules. And my parents weren't even upset?! All I have to say about that is "Well played, sister, well played."

On the car ride home, excitement filled Charlie's voice as she told us stories about her adventures and most importantly, all about the new love of her life—the Aussie Campbell. I could tell by Mom's silence that one of her worst fears had come true. Charlie had fallen in love with a boy continents and oceans away from our little home town of Deer Park, Ohio.

There was something about the glow that radiated from Charlie every time she said Campbell's name. The more she talked, the bigger grew the sinking feeling in the pit of my stomach. My sister had not only fallen in love with an Australian but she had met the man of her dreams—a kindhearted, funny, good-looking man who hadn't tried to tame her as all her past boyfriends had done but rather embraced her fearlessness. I somehow knew this wouldn't be the last time the family would be picking up Charlie from the airport. Looking back, I think that secretly Mom and Charlie both knew it too.

As Liz and Charlie giggled about Campbell, Mom and Dad remained silent, and I gently touched my belly and held back tears. Just as Charlie had kept Campbell a secret the entire three months that she was in Australia, I too had kept my own little secret from my family. Next fall I would not be following my dreams. I would not be moving away from home to attend college on the soccer scholarship I had worked so hard to earn. I, Emily Kathleen McCoy, was pregnant at the young age of eighteen.

After learning this fact, I had driven to several convenience stores within a twenty-mile radius to buy pregnancy test after pregnancy test only to confirm time and again what my gut already knew. After several weeks of denial and crying myself to sleep, I finally accepted the fact and adjusted my attitude from "This can't be my life" to "This is my life, and I need to take responsibility." And so I did.

While Charlie was living her dream in Australia and all my friends were enjoying the last half of their senior year, I found myself driving all over town looking for a second and then a third part-time job. On top of finishing my classwork and maintaining all the responsibilities that came with being class president, I worked seven days a week. After school let out, I'd head to a classmate's family business, an ambulance billing company. There I'd work from four thirty to eight thirty calling clients who had recently used their ambulance services. I'd gather the clients' insurance information and enter it into a computer system to bill their insurance companies. This was an amazing job to have as a high school student and paid very well.

On weekends I'd start my day off working at a local kids' gymnastics center where I'd host kids' birthday parties and then work the concession stand. After putting in eight hours there, I'd leave to go to my third and final job selling shoes at a shoe store. For a while I hid two of these jobs from Mom. I told her I was out living up my senior year with my girlfriends or at Dad's house.

In my "free time," instead of hanging out with my friends, I would go to different stores and price diapers, formula, and other baby needs to see who had the best deals. Instead of looking forward to going off to college and playing soccer, I faced the hard reality that college would have to wait. Instead of returning college soccer recruiters' phone calls, I hid in my room and cried over the fact that I'd never get to play college soccer while I searched the White Pages for local OB-GYNs. As I called various doctors' offices to see if they were accepting new patients, I was filled with overwhelming guilt. I knew I had to tell my parents, but I had been waiting for Charlie to return home. I didn't think my parents could handle the news while they were still worrying about Charlie being overseas.

After Charlie was home for a couple days, I sat my parents down and told them my secret. This was the first time I ever saw true disappointment in my parents' eyes but also the first time I realized that my parents' love was truly unconditional. They would love and support me no matter what I went through in life.

The Next Eight Years

I finished my senior year and graduated with high honors. The summer following graduation, while all my friends went on a trip to Cancun, I continued to work three jobs to save money. My nineteenth birthday came, and Apple, along with my gracious aunts, Patti and Anne, filled my birthday card with entirely too much money. I've never been one to accept handouts; however, I swallowed my pride and graciously accepted it. I realized I was going to need a great deal of help from my family. When fall rolled around, all my friends went off to college. Charlie went back to finish her final year at Denison, and Liz started her master of education program at Mount St. Joe. As for me, I painted the room I grew up in pink, turned it into a nursery, and on September 13 welcomed my sweet daughter Ellie into the world.

During Ellie's first year of life, my sole concern was to be the best mother I possibly could be. I quit all three of my jobs and lived off the money I had saved. My only responsibility was learning to be a mother and bonding with my daughter. This was the hardest but most rewarding year I've ever lived. Talk about a wake-up call! I was nineteen, living at home in the house I'd grown up in, and raising my own child with hardly any money to my name. My dream of going off to college on a soccer scholarship was now an unrealistic dream. I threw my old plans out the window and concentrated on coming up with new ones. Was I scared? More like petrified! Was I happy? When it came to being a mom I was extremely happy; however, in every other aspect of my life, no. For the first time in my life, I was quite the opposite of happy.

Not only was I a scared single mom but I was basically alone. Ellie's father was going to college full time and working part time. He and I tried to make things work, but in the end, I was deemed Ellie's custodial parent. When Ellie was a toddler, her father only made the effort to see her once or twice a month and would continue this pattern for the remainder of her childhood. All my friends were busy living their lives (at college). Yes, I saw and talked to them occasionally; however, we had all started different chapters of our lives. While I was starting the grow-up-and-figure-out-how-to-be-an-adult-and-a-mother chapter of my life, my friends were all starting the carefree drink-party-work-and-cram-for-exams chapter of their lives. I'm not saying they didn't have their own struggles or difficult times; they were just different worries than mine.

After college, Charlie moved back home to save money and to find a job then spent the next several years traveling weekly for work. In her free time she traveled to Australia to visit Campbell. When Liz wasn't at school, she was working and completing an internship.

Needless to say, I grew up fast over the next five years. The first year of Ellie's life, I was able to be a stay-at-home mom and became extremely close to my daughter. I fell totally in love with motherhood. However, every time I ventured out of the house to take Ellie for a walk, or to go to the grocery store, or to take Ellie to the park, I was under scrutiny. You would think that after living through my pregnancy looking like a thirteen-year-old pregnant girl rather than an eighteen-year-old, I'd be used to people's snide comments—but I wasn't. Every time I left the house, Ellie was with me, and every time we went out, someone had something to say about my age and immediately judged my parenting abilities. Whether it was a simple gasp or a "You look so young; you can't be more than thirteen" or a "That's your daughter, not your sister," strangers' comments never seemed to stop coming my way.

Right before Ellie's first birthday, I enrolled at the University of Cincinnati and was accepted to an off-campus branch just five minutes from Mom's house. The first two years of my college education, I was lucky enough to attend class there, which worked out perfectly for me. I was able to be with Ellie most of the day and take classes at night or on Saturday mornings. I was fortunate, too, to have Mom, Dad, Apple, and Patti to take care of Ellie while I was in class. Unfortunately, the money I had worked so hard to save eventually ran out, so I had to return to working a part-time job on top of balancing classes, homework, and raising Ellie. These were stressful and exhausting years; however, all of Ellie's smiles, laughs, hugs, and kisses were all the reward I needed to get through each day. I knew I was getting an education to give the both of us a better life, and she deserved my very best attempt. Looking back, I wouldn't have had it any other way. We had a special mother-daughter bond, and in many ways we grew up together.

For my last two years of college, I had to not only go to school year-round at the main campus, which was about twenty minutes from home, but my class schedule was a fixed schedule that included an unpaid internship as well. I no longer had the luxury of taking night and weekend classes and no longer had time to work a part-time job. At this point, Liz had finished her master's degree and was a teacher. Thankfully, because she had the summer off, she helped watch Ellie so I could attend my classes without worrying about how I would afford a full-time babysitter.

Those last two years of college were even harder than my first two, but with Mom, Dad, Apple, and Liz's help, I graduated when Ellie was five years old. Not only did I finish college but I graduated Magna Cum Laude. I earned a bachelor's degree in science, took my state boards, and was licensed in nuclear medicine and ultrasound. Immediately upon graduating, I landed a job at our local children's hospital. Being the size of a sixth-grader, I fit in well there. Not only had I done well in my education but so had Ellie. Her great-grandparents on her father's side had paid for her to attend an elite preschool. Ellie was excelling, and although she was the youngest in her class, she was placed a grade higher. Throughout the remainder of school, Ellie would continue to excel and test into advanced classes.

Thankfully, Ellie and I were able to live with Mom (now Nana) throughout my college years and for the first two years after graduation. With Dad (now Poppy) living just several streets away, he was always more than willing to help with Ellie in any way he could. Whether I needed their help to pick up Ellie from school or to get her to and from soccer or Taekwondo practice, I could always depend on them. Without my family's help, but especially Mom and Dad's help, I wouldn't have been a successful mother and college graduate.

When Ellie turned seven, I had saved enough money for a down payment on a house of my own. In June when Ellie's school let out, we packed up our belongings and moved out of the Glenbury home and into a new house four streets away—believe it or not, right next door to Poppy! Leaving the house that my sisters and I had grown up in and Ellie lived in for most of her childhood was bittersweet. That house holds so many memories of good times, bad times, childhood fights, childhood holidays, tears, laughter, and most importantly, a whole lot of love. However, I was beyond proud to be able to provide Ellie with a home to call our very own.

I took two weeks off to get settled into our new house. Those two weeks were amazing. Not only was I on cloud nine because I was an official homeowner but the local cable company had given us a free three-month subscription for being "new" to the neighborhood! I laugh because Ellie and I were definitely not new to Deer Park, but yes, we were new to the street, so we gladly accepted the free cable trial. Before then, I had never had the money to allow Ellie to watch Disney or Nickelodeon, so every night after dinner we popped popcorn, snuggled up, and binged on cable TV until we both fell asleep on the couch. In the middle of the night, I'd wake up and carry Ellie into her own bedroom then go upstairs to what used to be an attic (but the last owners had converted into a master suite). My own master suite! Having a home of my own was a surreal experience.

Many of the first nights in our home, I cried joyful tears as I drifted off to sleep and thought back to the days after Charlie had graduated from college and temporarily moved back to Mom's house. During this time, for almost a year while Charlie worked to save money to get a place of her own, I shared a bedroom with Ellie. I wanted Ellie to have a room of her own, so I kept her room the same but bought a trundle bed. After tucking her in at night, I'd wait until she was sound asleep and then pull out the trundle bed to sleep on.

For the second time in our lives Charlie and I were sharing a closet, only this time neither of us minded. In fact, while living together again in our childhood home, we became extremely close. We'd stay up late talking, we'd play with Ellie, go out to eat, and do all the things normal sisters do.

Even though I literally had no space to call my own, there was a roof over our heads, and we were in a safe, loving home, and that's all that mattered. I am forever indebted to my mom and dad.

During those eight years, Charlie and Liz faced their own struggles that came with being adults. They had their own problems, their own ups and downs, their own obstacles to overcome. Throughout the years, they'd offer to help with Ellie when they could to give me a break to spend time with my high school girlfriends, with whom I'm still close friends today. After Charlie moved out of Mom's, she found an apartment not too far away from Liz's.

Not only were there some difficult moments but there were some sad, heartbreaking ones as well. During those years, my family buried our sweet and loving Aunt Kay and our fun-loving and charismatic Uncle "Hudy." Sadly, we'd also cling to one another as we lay our dear grandma Apple to rest. Losing Apple was losing the most important piece of our family puzzle, our family glue. She was more than a grandma; she was our biggest fan and supporter. She was there for everything—dances, games, awards ceremonies. She was always on our side and never let us down. Although it is never easy to have a loved one pass, our family found a sense of peace in knowing that Apple had passed away peacefully in her sleep on Poppy's birthday. Although Poppy had passed when I was young, Apple never stopped loving him or keeping his memory alive. It was as if she didn't want another one of his birthdays to come and go without being in heaven with him.

Although we had trying times, us McCoy Boys still made time to enjoy life and have fun. As often as we could, we'd get together for dinners at Mom's, game night at Dad's, or hit the town for a girls' night out. My sisters were there to take me out and celebrate my twenty-first birthday. And when I turned twenty-five, we took an epic New Year's Eve trip to Las Vegas. All I can say about that trip is that I saw more random, crazy things in one night on the Las Vegas strip than I had ever seen in my entire sheltered twenty-five years of living in Deer Park, Ohio. When the crazy New Year's Eve adventure came to an end, I was ready to return home. We were there for one another to celebrate our accomplishments—such as graduating from college and landing our first real jobs—just as we were there to pick one another up from the letdowns that go along with becoming adults—such as breakups and fights with friends. Becoming adults was exciting and challenging, but luckily we had one another to remind us to laugh often and to live life to its fullest.

When Ellie turned eight, I met the man who would change our lives forever. After years of failed relationships (one long-term and several awful short-term relationships), I had given up on men and deemed myself to be a single mom for the rest of my life. I was more than happy raising Ellie on my own. However, one rainy November day, a man stood at a restaurant door, holding an umbrella built for two, and from that moment on, my heart was forever changed.

The first time I allowed KP into my home to meet Ellie, he brought her his old rock collection. They sat on the living floor for hours organizing rocks, talking, and laughing. The happiness on Ellie's face confirmed what my heart already knew: he was the one we'd been waiting for. One beautiful September day in 2013, I married him, and Ellie and I finally had not only a home but a complete family to call our own.

When One Door Closes, Dare to Dream!

Two years after I married, something happened that caused me to stop and think about my career and my future. At this time my job was using ultrasound technology to guide surgeons who operated on fetuses inside the womb. This was not only some of the most intense work I'd ever done but it was the most detailed and rewarding.

November 8, 2016, was a day I will never forget. After eight years of working at the same hospital and two years of specializing while receiving nothing but praise and promotion for a job well done, I learned that my duties were changing, and I was very unhappy with the change.

Growing up, everyone had encouraged me to follow my dreams, telling me I could accomplish anything I put my mind to as long as I dream big, but in reality I found that if our dreams seem to others to be too big, we receive little encouragement to pursue them. Not so with my husband. With his encouragement and a slight nudge, I came to believe that now was the perfect time for me to follow a dream I'd had for most of my life.

I'll never forget the blank expressions on my parents' faces as I explained my new life plan to them. We had just finished having Taco Tuesday at my house and were relaxing in the living room when I broke the news: "I'm quitting my job and focusing on a career in writing."

"I don't understand," Mom said with a worried expression on her face.

"What don't you understand?" I asked. I felt my explanation had been rather straightforward.

"You have a good career, and you make good money," Mom explained.

"I think what your mom is trying to say is why take a chance at losing everything when you've worked so hard to get where you are in life?" Dad argued for the both of them.

I understood why my parents were concerned. For years they had watched me struggle as a single mom while I worked very hard to pay for and earn my college education. After putting Ellie to bed at night, I'd stay up doing homework until the wee hours of the morning only to wake up at six o'clock in the morning and do it all again. Attending college and earning a degree had come at a high cost, so for me to put my job on hold in order to try my hand at writing seemed foreign and completely irrational to them.

"You guys taught me to always work on bettering myself—that no matter how challenging something seems, I have the power to make it a reality," I explained, my voice a little shaky now as I too was second-guessing my decision. I took a deep breath and reminded myself that I had made a decision, and now I needed to stick to it. "You also taught me to have faith. Having faith means believing in the unknown."

"I know we did," Mom said, "It's just—" she stammered, looking for the right words. "It's just that you never know what life will throw your way. Right now if, God forbid, anything were to happen to KP, you cannot financially support your family," she said as she reached for my hand and then added, "and you worked so hard to get to where you are today." Tears filled her eyes.

Dad pleaded, "Just make sure you're doing this for all the right reasons and not because you're upset with a decision that was made at work."

I swallowed hard as I tried to hold back tears and avoided looking Mom in the eyes. My life thus far had been far from conventional, so why should it be any different now? Was I making a huge mistake to change careers at this stage in my life? So many questions without answers filled my mind. But then I thought about the pile of black-and-white composition books I had kept throughout the years. Ever since fifth grade, I have always kept a pen and a blank book tucked inside my pillowcase. Every night I'd turn on my flashlight and instead of writing to my "dear diary" as most kids do, I would write poems, songs, and stories. I've always been able to lose myself in my writing—to get lost in a world that only existed in my mind. Hours would pass, and to me they seemed like minutes. I'd look at my clock and gulp because I knew I was going to be tired in the morning. I'd turn off my flashlight, tuck my book under my pillow, and force my mind to shut off for the night then I'd drift off to sleep thinking about my characters or humming a song I had composed.

Between graduating high school and getting married, writing had been put on hold because I was busy getting an education and being a mom, but now having a life partner who helped me to parent and manage household chores meant that many nights after tucking Ellie into bed, I had free time! For the first time in my adult life, I had time to do whatever I wanted to do, even if it was only for an hour or so each night. I bought a new composition book and began to write just as I had done all those years ago—at night and in bed. The only thing that had changed was that instead of writing by the light of a flashlight, I could keep my light on as late as I wanted, and I had a husband sitting next to me to share my stories with. Night after night, page after page, I began to fill a book with new stories, new adventures, and new life.

By the time I made the decision to leave the hospital, the story of my life as a McCoy Boy was exploding inside me. I knew that my childhood stories had been lying dormant just waiting for me to write them down. My hope is that I have written something that people all over the world will enjoy reading—that all my crazy life experiences have made you laugh and smile, and that I have inspired you to become the person you dream of becoming—the person you were meant to become.

Present Day

The ground is covered with snow in Cincinnati, Ohio, and icicles are hanging from the bare tree branches and roofs. It's Christmastime, and for the first time in several years, the McCoy Boys and all of our children are gathered at Nana's house, the same tri-level house on Glenbury Lane that we grew up in and will always know as home.

KP and I are happily married. We welcomed the newest member to our family, Ava, five months ago, and Ellie is now thirteen years old. When we first told Ellie we were expecting, she was far from thrilled. She locked herself in her room and refused to speak to either of us for an entire weekend. Now she proudly claims Ava as hers and is eager to help, except for when it comes to changing dirty diapers.

What about the other McCoy Boys? Well, Liz, who struggled the most in school, is the only one of us to get a master's degree. She earned her degree in early childhood education and works at a local elementary school. She fell in love with a cop and was the first one of us to marry. Liz didn't move far from Glenbury Lane. She's a quick five-minute car drive away from Nana and Poppy. Not only is she happily married but she is a proud mom to two boys and a girl!

And Charlie? Wouldn't you know, the gut feeling I had all those years ago when the family picked her up from the airport that first time was right. She married that Aussie Campbell and followed her dreams and heart and moved to Australia. As luck would have it, her Cincinnati employer at the time was able to transfer her to a branch in Australia. Funny how things just fall into place for some people. Campbell and Charlie have a curly-haired, green-eyed girl that's six months older than Ava.

Charlie's decision to move to Australia was one of the hardest things our family went through. The older we grew, the closer us McCoy Boys became. When the Aussies aren't here in Ohio, a void fills all of our hearts and lives, but whenever they do come to visit, our entire family feels complete.

It has been several years since we've all been together for Christmas. After all the excited chaos of the grandchildren tearing open their presents, the boys happily play with their new toys and the younger girls lie down for naps. Finally, the adults have time to relax and reminisce.

While Charlie, Liz, and I turn on the Charlie Brown Christmas music, pour a glass of wine and "cheers" one another, Ellie searches the fridge for something to snack on.

"Ugh, Mom, when are we going to eat? I'm so hungry." Ellie moans.

"Soon, my impatient teen," I reassuringly tease her.

"I can make you a quick snack," Aunt Charlie offers Ellie with a mischievous grin on her face.

"Like what?" I suspiciously ask, knowing that look all too well.

She looks towards Liz and smiles. Liz nods back, knowing exactly what Charlie is thinking.

"Hey El, did we ever tell you about some of the games we used to play with your mom?" Liz asks.

"Um, I don't think so," Ellie answers as she shuts the refrigerator door.

"We used to play this really fun game called Concoction." Charlie tells her.

Liz, Charlie, and I all look at one another and begin to laugh.

"Oh, no!" I protest, as Charlie and Liz carry on laughing.

"What's so funny?" Ellie insists we fill her in on the inside joke.

After being filled in on the "rules" of Concoction, Ellie thinks it's hilarious and agrees to try it.

"Let me remind you," I say as Liz eagerly blindfolds Ellie and Charlie happily heads towards the refrigerator to grab her ingredients, "that my daughter is older than all your kids, and what goes around comes around! So don't come complaining to me when Ellie wants to play this game years from now with your kids!"

"Aunt Liz, Aunt Charlie, tell me more about the games you used to play with Mom," Ellie asks as she sits blindfolded waiting to be spoon fed her next creation.

"Did your Mom ever tell you about how we would chase her with Poppy's smelly socks?" Liz asks.

"No!" Ellie laughs even harder.

"Or how we used to make her take a bath with the dog?"

Ellie's laughing so hard she can't even respond.

"Okay, okay, let's not give her any ideas for her baby sister," I say as I give my sisters the watch-what-you-tell-her look.

"Tell me more!" Ellie insists.

So here we sit at the same kitchen bar we used to sit at as three little girls, then as children, then as teenagers, and now as grown adults, reminiscing on growing up McCoy Boys—the games we played, the vacations we went on, the fights we had, and all the mischievous things we did with and without getting caught. Liz, Charlie, and I look at one another as we tell Ellie all our stories with smiles on our faces but with sadness in our eyes. The years have passed without our realizing how quickly we grew into adults.

We spend our childhood wishing time away—"I can't wait to be tall enough to ride that ride," "I can't wait to be old enough to drive," "I can't stand Mom's rules," "I can't wait to live on my own"—and then one day we wake up and realize all those things we couldn't wait to do, we've now done. We're no longer children, but adults. Adulthood can bring many amazing things—marriage, traveling, making up your own rules—however, it can also bring what seems to be never-ending responsibility—working to pay bills, taking care of your health, taking care of your pets, taking care of your children, taking a job you might not want but find yourself needing, cleaning your home, keeping up the yard work—

and some days you find yourself envying the days when you were a kid with no responsibilities or cares in the world. You find yourself wishing you were a kid again. You remember the feeling of being out of school for an entire summer with nothing else to do but hang out with your friends, or being able to sleep in on weekends and not having to be anywhere at a certain time, or having slumber parties with friends and staying up all night without worrying about how tired you'll be the next day. But mostly you embrace life as most kids do believing you are invincible—that nothing bad can happen to you as long as Mom or Dad is by your side.

Looking back, what I wouldn't give to relive some of those awful games my sisters played to torture me. We only lived together in our childhood home on Glenbury Lane for a short period of our lives. Now we're grown, and life has taken us in different directions—off to live our own adventures and start families and lives of our own. We all are happy and we all love our families, but some days we miss just being kids. I even miss when we were crazy, hormonal teenage girls trying to figure out life and who we were as individuals.

I was born to two loving parents and two sisters who never wanted me. Throughout the years, Liz and Charlie teased me, tortured me, taught me many life lessons, laughed with me, cried with me, and in their own odd way, loved me immensely. Despite everything my sisters put me through I grew up to be a proud, loving mother and wife, an aunt, and through my job helped countless sick children. All in all, I think I turned out okay. I wouldn't trade my life or my family for anything. These crazy stories are the stories I know as my memories, my childhood, my life. I am Emily Kathleen McCoy, and I survived growing up McCoy. Now, as adults, my sisters and I can't survive without one another.

THE END

Made in the USA
Columbia, SC
15 June 2019